Deserter

A novel based on true events

Ann Barrie

156 Owhiro Bay Parade,
Wellington 6023,
New Zealand

ann.barrie.nz@gmail.com

Cover design by Justine Elliott

National Library of New Zealand
Cataloguing-in-Publication Data
Barrie, Ann, 1947–
Deserter : a novel based on true events / Ann Barrie.
ISBN 978-0-473-39065-5 (pbk.)
ISBN 978-0-473-39066-2 (epub)
1. World War, 1939–1945—Campaigns—Fiction. 2. Naval convoys—
North Atlantic Ocean—History—20th century—Fiction. I. Title.
NZ823.3—dc 23

To Chris King
Royal Navy no. P/JX310293

And to all the men, of any nationality, who
served in the Arctic convoys of World War II.

Also, in loving memory of my father
Charles MacKenzie Herbert
1921–2009
NZ Army & RNZAF no. 4211709

And my husband
William Glen Barrie
1930–2015
British Army no. 22127250
NZ Army no. 37739

CHAPTER 1

Keith Mathieson had been swimming for some time and was well out from the shore. As he turned facedown again, he watched his hand cut cleanly through the water in front of him. With the rotation of his torso, the other hand pulled back behind him and rose forward in an arc before in its turn cutting into the water, fingers soft. Again his body rotated, and he turned his head to breathe. Each stroke seemed to push behind him not just the water, but the dust, the dryness and the scream of exploding shells. His whole body felt good in the cool embrace of the sea.

He moved in an easy rhythm. He could have gone on forever. But it was time to head back. He changed direction and swam to the rickety jetty. Holding on with one hand, he submerged completely, moving his head from side to side with his mouth open. The brine hit his tongue and the roof of his mouth. Then he surfaced and swung himself up to where Jimmy sat. The two of them had hiked here first thing, soon after the sun inched above the horizon.

"I thought you'd ne'er return," Jimmy grumbled. "Where did you learn to swim like that?"

"Edinburgh. After my Da sent me to live with my aunt." As he shook the water off his hair, Keith thought back to that period of his life. He was fourteen and finding it difficult to bear the death of his mother. His father had sent him away to live with his Ma's sister, who had married well and lived in a big house. She had paid for him to attend school for another year and also arranged swimming lessons at a nearby pool. He grew to love the feeling of his muscles in motion, driving his body through the water.

"I miss my Da," Jimmy said. "He was a lorry driver. Used to take me out wi' him sometimes when I was a wee lad. Once we went away overnight, stopped at a cafe for breakfast. Bacon and eggs and black puddin' and cups of tea." He smiled at the memory. "After my Da died it was just Ma and me and my brother, Donald. When all this is over we're going to open a garage together, back in Inverness."

They lapsed into companionable silence. Keith thought of his own father: proud Highlander, slow to show emotion, and disapproving of everything he did. The two of them had drifted apart since his mother died.

"So this is where you went." Two men from their unit, Scottie and Mack, were walking along the jetty towards them.

Keith and Jimmy shuffled along in their seat so the other two could settle down beside them. Scottie passed around cigarettes, and the four men sat quietly, faces upward to exhale into the sky. It was as blue as could be except for some gauzy strokes of white that were painted above the sun as if with a wide watercolour brush.

Several minutes passed, then Scottie blew a perfect ring of smoke up into the air and said casually, "How long do ye lads think it wuid take me to get to Cairo?"

"Got a girl there, have you? Or you'd like to have a girl there?" Keith laughed. "Sorry, laddie. You'll have to wait. The only place you're going is back into the desert."

Scottie, short and wiry, assumed a look of bravado. "That's just it. I'm no' goin' back. I've had enough of that shithole. There's lots of lads in Cairo holed up wi' braw lassies."

"Braw lassies who'll give them the clap," said Jimmy. "Yer no' talk'n about deserting?"

"Aye. Want to keep me company?"

Jimmy shook his head.

"No' worth it, laddie," Keith said. "This R and R by the sea has made your brain mushy. Once you're in the thick of it again, you won't have time to think. You'll just follow orders, use your instincts to stay alive like a wee animal, and calm your nerves with cigarettes."

Mack had been listening in silence. Now he spoke up. "How do you plan to get there?" His voice had a sharp edge to it, but Scottie appeared not to notice.

"Hitchhike."

Mack gave a short laugh. "You're a fucking idiot. You'd never reach Cairo. Even if you did, you'd get caught. Do you really want to go to the Glasshouse?"

Keith and Jimmy exchanged glances. It was common knowledge that Mack had spent a month in the notorious Mustafa Barracks soon after they all arrived in Egypt with the 51st Highland Division—something to do with striking an officer; but he never talked about it.

Scottie still had a defiant expression.

"Listen carefully," Mack continued. "I will tell you this once and once only. The Glasshouse means sadistic bastards of screws who grab every opportunity to humiliate you. Being called yellow if you're a deserter. Doing everything at the double. Endless drills and meaningless tasks, hour after hour in the bloody sun. Forbidden to speak to other prisoners. Eight of you in a stinking cell." He paused for breath. "Let's just say I'd rather risk being blown apart than go back there."

Keith stared at Mack in stunned silence. Neither of the other two said a word.

Mack shrugged. "Let's go for a stroll, Scottie. See you other boys later."

Scottie stood up without a word and followed Mack off the jetty.

"Nae danger of Scottie running away any day soon," Keith said.

Jimmy looked at Keith, his head cocked to one side. "Would you ever …?"

"Nah."

"You're in for twelve years, aren't you?"

"Aye. Got me off the streets."

Keith studied the water. It was very clear, blemished only by a cigarette packet floating past. "Time for you to get your baws wet, laddie. Off ye go." He gave Jimmy a nudge.

Jimmy slid slowly into the water and dog-paddled around in circles near the jetty, an expression of fierce concentration on his face.

Keith observed once again how thin his shoulders were. He had first become aware of this in Cairo when they had the rare opportunity to take a shower. Jimmy had asked Keith to massage his shoulders, which had become stiff from all the driving, and Keith had rubbed them tentatively, feeling the bones fragile beneath his fingers. "Firmer," Jimmy had instructed. And then, "Ouch, that's too hard. Didna' ye used to rub each other's backs in the bath?"

No, they did not. Keith's mother had bathed his brother and him when they were very young; however, once they grew older, the whole family had bathed in swift succession in the tub that was set in front of the fire once a week. They were a close family, at least while his mother was still alive, but physically undemonstrative with each other.

Keith watched Jimmy circling by the jetty, then he laughed, "That looks like hard work. Come on, I'll give you a hand up." He reached down to Jimmy and grasped him firmly.

The two young men sat on the jetty for a while longer, their legs dangling into the water, easy in each other's company. Keith breathed slowly and deeply. After everything they had gone through during the battles at El Alamein, these few days of rest and recreation were good.

"So where do ye think we're pushin' on to next?" Jimmy asked. "Tunisia?"

"Maybe." Keith said. "Or what about somewhere further south?" Kicking Jimmy on the leg, he quoted:

> *A masculine maid from Khartoum*
> *Took a ladylike boy to her room.*
> *They spent the whole night*
> *In one helluva fight*
> *As to which would do what, and to whom.*

Jimmy gave him a shove in the shoulder. "Away an' bile yer heid. Let's go back now."

They trudged across the sand to the tents where their platoon was housed. That evening they and some of the other men had a singsong in the mess tent. Warmly clad against the cold night air, they sang all the songs they knew, ending with "Hielan' Laddie".

Where ha' ye been a' the day?
Bonnie laddie, Hielan' laddie
Saw ye him that' far awa'
Bonnie laddie, Hielan' laddie.

The men fell silent. Jimmy, watching their faces, which had become sombre, picked up his mouth organ and played a cheerful jig.

The men applauded, asking for more.

Keith smiled. He liked it when Jimmy got the chance to shine.

Three months later, Keith and Mack were being transported in the back of a Bren Gun Carrier along with some equipment. Jimmy was up front in the driver's seat with the sergeant beside him. The vehicle was travelling slowly. Keith knew that Jimmy would be concentrating intently, straining his eyes in the dark to follow the tiny light at the rear of the vehicle ahead. It was always noisy in these carriers, with a lot of stopping and starting. They were all tired, had been since they got up that morning and shook the scorpions out of their clothes and boots.

Mack had not mentioned the Glasshouse again since that day in November. Keith was as close to him as anyone, because he and Mack were the two-man Bren Gun team for the platoon. Keith was the gunner, responsible for carrying and firing the twenty-two pound light machine gun; Mack was his loader, always beside him with extra magazines. He was Keith's third loader. The first man had gone near mad from the heat and the lack of water in the desert. The second man had his foot blown off. Keith had hoisted him over his shoulder and carried him to safety.

Keith coughed as the dust caught the back of his throat. Dust, sand, grit. In your clothes. Up your nostrils. In your eyes. In your gun. He had spent time the previous evening stripping his Bren Gun and cleaning the parts with an oily rag. He had done this so many times that he could have stripped it with his eyes closed. His eyes must have started closing now, because he felt himself suddenly jerk awake. He did not want to fall asleep; he wanted to stay alert, just like Jimmy needed to be when he was driving. For want of anything else to focus on, he started stripping his gun in his mind, working through the steps. *Push out the body-locking pin. Slide the body group to the rear as far as it will go.* His head jerked forward again and he forced himself awake. *Give a quick jerk on the cocking lever to move the piston group to the rear. Remove the piston and breechblock from the gun, and take the breechblock off the piston.* This was taking longer than he expected. Usually his fingers did the work automatically without him thinking about the steps. *Raise the barrel nut catch, push the barrel forward and remove it. Hold the body and slide off the butt. Turn the body to the left to remove it from the bipod.*

That was enough. He did not have the energy to reassemble the gun. He glanced across at the shadowy outline of Mack. He had dozed off. Up front, Sergeant would be talking to Jimmy, keeping an eye on him.

Sergeant MacFarlane was a decent bloke and like a father figure, dishing out advice on everything from technical matters to safe sex. "You know what this is for, don't you?" he had said during one of his talks, holding a French letter dangling from his fingers.

Keith had replied, "Aye, I know that much at least. It's for putting over the tip of my weapon to keep out the dust."

"Cheeky bugger," Sergeant had guffawed.

Keith flexed his shoulders. *This night air would freeze the balls off a brass monkey.* Gradually his eyes closed and his head jolted forward.

All at once the monotonous progress of the Bren Carrier

changed. First they turned a slight corner. Another vehicle was approaching, and the carrier veered to one side.

And then, a deafening explosion, followed by an agonised cry.

Chapter 2

North Africa
February 1943

Keith groaned and tried to open his eyes. They were heavy. Everything was heavy. Someone gently lifted his head and inserted something between his lips. He swallowed with a gulp. Cool water. Then he drifted away. Sometime later he woke again. Everything hurt. He managed to open his eyes. Where was he? The air was hot and still, but he heard the light flapping of canvas.

A shadowy figure approached, and then a nurse bent over him.

"Welcome back, soldier. You've been out of it for two days." Her voice was bright.

Keith tried to speak but could not move his jaw.

The nurse understood. "I can tell you what happened. I was here when they brought you in." She spoke slowly. "You were in a Bren Carrier that ran over a landmine. You were thrown clear. Your jaw is broken. It's all wired up. That's why you have trouble opening your mouth. You suffered a concussion too." She lifted his head, pushing a straw between his lips.

Keith sipped the water and then let the straw drop. He moved his head from side to side, trying to see the other beds. *Where is Jimmy?*

Again the nurse understood. "Are you looking for the men who were on the carrier with you?"

Keith nodded.

The nurse did not answer immediately and Keith, watching her face, knew what she was going to say.

She took his hand and said gently, "The other three were killed. I'm sorry."

Keith spent the next few days staring at the screen window of the hospital tent or sleeping. Sleeping mostly. Doctors visited occasionally. Nurses and orderlies helped him eat and drink, tended to his needs. Even after he recovered enough to get out of bed and stroll around outside, he felt tired and listless and disinclined to chat to other people.

One day he discovered a stray dog behind a tent on the perimeter of the camp. Next morning he went there again. He was trying to entice the little mongrel with a titbit of food when he heard a voice behind him.

"That mutt looks as if she could do with a decent feed."

Keith turned around to see who had spoken. A tall, powerfully built man with ginger colouring and short-cropped curly hair stood leaning on a crutch.

"Aye, she does," Keith said.

The man with the crutch held out his hand. "Joe McDonald. Aussie. You're Scottish, I reckon."

Keith clasped Joe's hand. "Keith Mathieson." Then he gestured at the dog. "She reminds me of the wee terrier I had when I was a lad. Betty."

"Christ, mate! What sort of a name's that for a dog?"

Keith laughed. "Don't tell me. You have a dog with a male-sounding name?"

"Yeah. Digger. Half dingo. He's got a prodigious appetite. Once he's finished his own tucker he'll steal anything within range. Sausages, lamb chops, batch of nutties left on the kitchen table."

"Betty had her moments. She saved my life once."

"'Struth!"

"I was just a bairn, about three. We were having a picnic. I wandered off and next moment I was facedown in a stream. Betty had followed me and she started barking frantically. My father fished me out."

"One of my mates in Aussie had a similar tale, but it was the other way round: he saved his dog's life. The old mutt had been swimming in the river, and my mate suddenly realised he was floating on his back with his paws in the air. He hauled him out and gave him mouth to mouth. The dog had another year of dozing in the sun before he passed away again—permanently this time."

"What about Digger? Still alive and well?"

"Oh yeah. He disappeared for two days when I joined the army, and the family thought he'd gone walkabout. But do you know where he was? Lying on the floor, on the far side of my bed. Fancy him going without his tucker for that long." Joe looked reflective. "My sister's minding him. She said his appetite's not what it used to be. He can only manage two meat pies at a sitting."

Keith and Joe lay on their backs under the olive trees, smoking cigarettes and listening to the sounds of the night: the chirp of a bird somewhere nearby, men's voices raised in laughter, occasional camels being driven by. They had become good friends and spent a lot of time together yarning about sport, food, girls, Scottish history (Joe's paternal grandfather had come from Glasgow) and how they looked forward to rejoining their units. Joe was a clever bugger, had studied history at university, but he played this down.

Joe stubbed out his cigarette and then rolled towards Keith and propped himself up on one elbow, peering at something beyond Keith's torso. "Have a gander at this, mate. They've put on a show for us."

Keith sat up and looked. In a nearby tent, women's naked bodies were silhouetted, dark shadows raising their arms above their heads, rubbing shoulders and backs.

"Aren't they generous, letting sex-starved soldiers observe them having their sponge baths," Joe said.

The two men watched until the light was extinguished, and then they rolled on to their backs again and lit more cigarettes.

Joe looked across at Keith. "You're quiet, mate."

Keith shrugged his shoulders. "I didn't sleep very well last night."

After tossing and turning for hours, he had fallen into a fitful sleep only to find haunting images of his brother, from a day nine years ago, surfacing in his mind. Duncan was eleven and he was twelve and a half. The two of them and their friends Fraser and Alick lay on their stomachs peering down into a deep well, the water at the bottom and something floating there.

"D'ye ken what it is?"

"A sheep's head?"

"Nah, too small."

"A lamb's head?"

"A bogill?"

"Let's see if we can hit it."

Keith picked up a stone and threw it down. It landed beside the object with a distant *plop*, causing dark ripples of water to swell out from it. Pleased with his success, he fetched a rock. He held it in both hands, down near his knees, and heaved it into the water. The rock made a deep splash, the sound of which resonated around the sides of the well.

"Wow!"

The object was pushed out of sight by the rock until it bobbed to the surface again.

Duncan looked across at Keith, and then got up and sauntered away. He returned, staggering under the weight of a boulder. He had just reached the perimeter of the well when he stumbled and pitched forward headfirst, still carrying the large rock. Keith heard a loud cry. He did not know if it came from Duncan or himself. Rooted to the ground, he watched as Duncan disappeared into the well. Now he heard nothing. Everything had become unreal, not part of him at all.

All at once the noise rushed back. Behind him someone

whimpered, and beside him a voice called, "Keith, Keith. What shall we do?"

Keith shook his head to clear it, and then he wriggled forward and stared down. He knew at once what needed to be done. "Run and get help," he ordered Fraser. "Tell 'em to bring a rope." As Fraser ran to do his bidding, Keith said to Alick, "Ye wait here. I'm going down." With that, he half climbed, half slid down the side of the well.

Duncan's body lay crumpled at the bottom, facedown in water that proved to be shallow, not even up to Keith's knees. He crouched in the dank darkness, supporting his brother's bleeding head. He was numb, his body and his feelings frozen. Duncan made no sound, no sign he was still alive.

The men arrived with ropes and they hauled up Duncan's limp body. Then they lifted Keith to the surface and wrapped him in blankets.

Duncan never regained consciousness, and the inquest determined the cause of his death to be a large fracture to the skull and a bleed on the brain. Keith's parents said no one was to blame, but he felt responsible. If Duncan had not been trying to impress him, he would never have fallen.

He did not talk to anyone about it. What was there to say?

Chapter 3

Northwest Atlantic
June 1943

There was a heavy sea, and a cool wind whipped and tugged at Keith as he made his way across the open deck. He stepped over the barge hatch into shelter and then, lurching a little, continued down the steps. Below in the troop deck there was always warmth to be found, along with the smell of stale air and sweat.

Greatcoats and kitbags hung from hooks in the roof. By the far wall were long tables and seats that had been hurriedly wiped down after the midday meal, and above them hammocks had been tied up and arched in the middle. As Keith reached the foot of the steps he could see figures huddled around an old army blanket spread out on the floor. It was the crown and anchor school. The board with its six squares was laid flat in the centre, a coin on each square, but the eyes of those around the board were fixed on the man with the dice box.

Joe McDonald had a good patter and his voice held the school as he coaxed and promised, entreated and challenged. "Come on, mates. Lay your bets. You're playing with an honest firm. I'll pay you." He squatted by the side of the blanket as the dice box rattled. "Cactus Joe's the name. We'll take anything from a tanner to a quid." All the time, his eyes roved over the group.

For a second Joe glanced in Keith's direction and Keith caught the slight pursing of his lips. Business must not be so good today.

Keith and Joe had been among the original founders of the school, and had pooled their funds and gambled together until sufficient players had come in. Joe assumed a different moniker for each game. *"Cactus Joe" suits him*, Keith thought. *He can be a prickly bugger.* He had a persuasive manner too, and a cool, calm cheek. When they were discharged from hospital, they were recommended for light work around base, but Joe had somehow wangled them this job escorting prisoners of war on a ship bound for Canada.

The crown and anchor school was dragging a little, and he had a headache, so Keith made his way towards his hammock. He glanced at the porthole beside him. It was open; but at night, with the blackout, it was screwed tightly shut and the air below would grow hot and stuffy. He loosened the rope round the middle of the hammock and swung himself into it. He wriggled his body into a comfortable position and turned his head to one side, swaying gently, so he could watch a soldier, Butters, who was playing patience at the table below.

After persevering for a while, Butters groaned and started to reassemble the pack. "One of these days I'll get this to work out right. I need a change of scenery to refresh the old brain." He shuffled the cards languidly, gazing up at Keith. "I wonder how much leave we'll be given in Canada, Jock. I hope they don't confine us to port."

"As far as I'm concerned, the quicker we turn around the better. But I hope we get our mail there and they don't hold it till we're back with our units."

"You know, Jock, all you think about is your mail. Remember that bundle you got from your girl just before we sailed? She must have written to you every week. And you bloody well sorted them into date order before you read them." The ship started to roll, as it swung side-on to the swell. Butters leaned forward and looked up at the swaying hammock. "What's she like?"

"The girl who writes to me?" He was not going to tell Butters that she was his second cousin, four years younger than him. They had grown up in neighbouring houses, and the two families were close. Instead he said, "Slender legs, lovely figure, long brown hair and a soft voice."

Butters drew a shapely figure in the air and started singing, "I know a lassie. A bonnie Highland lassie. She's as pure as the—"

He ducked to one side to avoid the book Keith hurled at him.

"Knock it off. You Sassanachs are all the same. No appreciation of the feelings that flow from a man's heart. Just give you a pint of beer, some fish and chips and a dart board, and you're content."

Butters put down his cards and chanted:

> *There was a young Scot in Madrid*
> *Who got fifty-five fucks for a quid.*
> *When they said, "Are you faint?"*
> *He replied, "No, I ain't,*
> *But I don't feel as good as I did."*

"Not me," Keith said. "I've got finesse." Swinging back and forth he quoted:

> *There was a young athlete named Grimmon*
> *Who developed a new way of swimmin':*
> *By a marvellous trick*
> *He would scull with his prick,*
> *Which attracted loud cheers from the women.*

Butters roared, "I can do better than—"

"Are you giving as good as you get, mate?" broke in Joe, who had just arrived. He stared out the open porthole, shaking his head. "It's a shame. All this liquid and not a bloody drop to drink." He turned to Keith. "When we do strike port, son, we'll make the town sit up. After the desert and now the friggin' ocean, I've developed a thirst."

Chapter 4

Halifax, Nova Scotia
June 1943

The tide was full in when the ship berthed, and it towered above the pier. Keith and Joe stepped side-on down a gangway that was slippery and inclined at a sharp angle. They both had small haversacks slung over their shoulders.

They had been paid the night before; and the money, when added to their winnings from the crown and anchor school, would ensure them a good time. It seemed they would be in port for several days. There were prisoners of war to disembark and stores and cargo to load, and then they would need to wait for a convoy to assemble before they could head back across the Atlantic. Keith had intended to return to the ship at night, but Joe had once again been persuasive.

"Listen, son," he said. "We'll see enough of this old tub before we've finished with it. Let's spend a night or two ashore in a decent bed for a change. We'll stow some stuff in a haversack and be prepared for a stay."

It was easier to agree than to argue with Joe, and so Keith packed some gear.

After wandering around the town for an hour or so—it was very quiet—they searched for a place where they could eat. In a side street they came across a services canteen. There was a cheerful hum of conversation inside, and servicemen in a variety of uniforms sat at long tables and small, round tables.

The meal smelt appetising as Keith and Joe lined up with

their trays. There was white bread, plenty of butter, real milk and a tempting hot meal: chicken and gravy and mashed potato. They had not seen anything like this for a long time.

They collected their food and made their way to a table where Joe had sighted the dark blue uniform of two Australian airmen. One was tall and thin with brown hair combed back from his face and a slight droop to this mouth. He stared listlessly across the table. His companion had neatly trimmed reddish-blonde hair and a ready smile.

The shorter man looked up as Keith and Joe approached, giving them a friendly nod. "I'm Blue," he said. "And this streak of misery is Stretch."

Keith and Joe introduced themselves and sat down at the table. The food tasted good, so Joe had almost finished his meal before he spoke. He glanced at each Aussie in turn and then addressed Stretch. "When does this town wake up, mate? It's a bit quiet at the moment."

Stretch lifted his eyes. "Halifax died long ago. Too many uniforms."

"What about women?"

"Women! If there are any decent women in this town their mothers have put them under lock and key. Those on the loose are dogs."

"Well, after ten days at sea, I'm not proud. I could do a line with that dame any day," said Joe, indicating a young apron-clad woman who was clearing tables.

"She's all yours, mate. We're leaving town this afternoon."

"Aren't you two stationed here?" Keith asked.

The Aussie stirred and stretched. "Hell no!" He relaxed and dropped his elbow on to the table, then continued in a flat tone, "We're at a manning depot further west, hanging round waiting for a course."

"What are you both?"

"What are we?" Blue said. "Well, we've already done army service in Papua New Guinea. We transferred to the air force back in Aussie and did our preliminary training there. We hope to be pilots one day, but meanwhile we're AWOL. We got fed up hanging round so we hopped over the back fence."

Keith was sceptical. "As easy as that? What will your Air Force say about it?"

"The Canadians run our training here, under the Empire Air Training Scheme. I don't think the Royal Canadian Air Force will worry too much about us so long as we're on the spot when they finally need us for a posting. We're a headache to them when we're bored, a bad example to new recruits."

Keith chuckled. "I can imagine."

"You know, they've got a regulation that whenever you pass the bloody flagpole, you salute the flag. We thought it was a bit of a joke at first, but they started to get strict about it. So one night after the boys had a few drinks in town, they came back and—"

"Chopped down the flagpole." A Canadian had joined the group. He winked at Keith and said in an undertone, "That's the second time I've heard that tale from an Aussie and I've also heard it from a Newzie. That flagpole must go up and down an awful lot."

Undeterred at the interruption, Blue continued, "Well, after that they did their best to keep us out of the way."

"Very wise of them," the Canadian said. "But now you've granted yourselves leave, how will you know when you're needed for posting?"

"No worries, mate. Within twenty-four hours of word coming out about a posting or a pay parade, the grapevine will let us know."

Joe asked the Canadian what he was doing at the moment, and he said he had completed his training as a navigator and was waiting for a troop ship to take him to England. He chatted for a while until he spotted a friend, then he wandered off again. The rest of the party lapsed into silence. Joe's eyes still followed the waitress. Stretch picked up a fork and started to tap up and down on the table.

"You mentioned you were leaving this afternoon. Where will you head?" Keith asked.

The fork continued to tap on the cloth. "A little jaunt across the border into the States. There are plenty of towns over there where strange uniforms are a novelty, and open sesame to hospitality."

"Come with us if you like," Blue said.

"Nah, mate. Count me out," Joe replied, with another glance at the waitress. "I'm going to stick around." He got to his feet and meandered over to the young woman.

Keith took longer to respond. They had been instructed not to leave the port area; but, on the other hand, the ship would be here for several days and the idea of visiting the States intrigued him. The place had a touch of glamour about it. With his crown and anchor winnings, he had a reasonable amount of money.

"Come on," Stretch said. "Your mate won't worry about you tonight. I don't fancy his chances with this chick—the goods in the canteen aren't for handling—but he'll get his shoes under some other sheila's bed."

That's true, Keith thought. *I'll be hanging round Halifax by myself.* He had already worked out from their time together at the hospital that Joe had a roving eye.

He had only had one sexual experience himself. It was September 1942, a month after Keith and Jimmy had arrived in Egypt with their platoon. Emboldened by alcohol, they had confided to Sergeant that they wanted to visit a Cairo brothel. Soon after, Keith had found himself strolling with Sergeant and Jimmy down a busy avenue where trams, carts, army trucks and pedestrians vied for space.

Sergeant led them off the avenue into a narrow street lined with shops and sheltered by canvas awnings. The humid air was filled with the fragrance of spices, colognes and incense, and they were swept along in a swarming flow of men in fezzes and caftans. He stopped in front of a tall, whitewashed building and gestured to Keith and Jimmy to follow him.

They entered straight into a large, carpeted salon furnished with a scattering of chairs and a long sofa covered with an embroidered cloth. To left and right, narrow stairs led up to a balcony, at the rear of which were half a dozen doors, all closed but one.

Sergeant spoke to the brothel Madam, then at Sergeant's prompting, Jimmy followed a scantily clad girl up the stairs. Keith and Sergeant waited on the sofa.

One of the doors opened and a red-faced soldier descended the stairs, still buttoning his fly. After a few minutes a woman emerged on to the balcony. She wore a flimsy, almost transparent robe through which her full breasts showed. She laid her hand on the railing and looked down at them. Her eyes were large and dark, her skin a creamy olive colour, and her luxuriant black hair was swept up at the back of her head. She was not young.

"Off you go," Sergeant whispered.

Keith climbed the stairs and followed the woman to a small room, which was decorated with patterned wallpaper. He closed the door rather uncertainly, then paused just inside the room, unsure what to do next. His eyes darted around and he saw a bed, a clothes rack, a dressing table, a wooden chair, and a basin and pitcher. Drifting into the room from outside were the sounds of laughter, shouts, accordion music, singing and the braying of animals. The woman, still with her back to him, reached across to close the window. He noticed she had ample buttocks.

She undressed herself, tossing her robe on to the wooden clothes rack, and turned towards him. Keith smelled the woman's musky perfume, looked shyly at her face. Her skin was smooth and she had painted eyebrows. He lowered his gaze, staring transfixed at her pubic mound. It was shaved bare beneath her soft, round belly. He might have stood there forever, but the woman spoke

"My name is Samia," she said, in heavily accented English.

Twenty minutes later, he joined Jimmy on the sofa downstairs to wait for Sergeant. Jimmy's cheeks were flushed, and he felt his own face burning. Up there in the room, Samia had pleasured him in a way that quickly aroused him. She was patient with his youthful fumbling and nervous excitement, but he had no idea what she thought of it all. She was inscrutable.

The turnaround at the brothel was brisk. Four soldiers entered the salon, talking noisily, then flopped down to await their turn.

Sergeant emerged from one of the upstairs rooms and joined Keith and Jimmy, asking, "Mission accomplished?"

They both nodded.

In Keith's mind, that is what it was: he and Jimmy had not wanted to die virgins. It was also an experience separate from his real life. His real life was an enclosed world of male camaraderie, discipline and danger.

Keith looked at Joe, and then at Blue and Stretch, torn between obeying the rules and experiencing something interesting and different. He felt almost panicky at the prospect of making a decision.

Stretch raised an eyebrow. "You don't need his permission, do you?"

Keith felt his face redden and he said in a rush, "I'll come with you. When do we leave?"

Blue reached for his cigarette case. "We'll catch the train out this evening and head south. Once we get near the border we'll take to the road and make use of the thumb. There'll be plenty of traffic going down that way."

Chapter 5

The train was waiting at Halifax station, the eastern terminus for a long railway line. Keith settled himself into a seat opposite Blue and Stretch, gazing out the window at the hustle and bustle on the platform. Family groups said their farewells; railway officials marched up and down with their check-boards; and, above all, clusters of servicemen—soldiers, sailors, airmen—heaved kitbags, smoked cigarettes and called out to each other. The steam from the locomotive mingled with the mist in the damp evening air as a steady stream of people climbed on board, lifting suitcases, packs and heavy coats on to the overhead racks.

Finally the locomotive gave a muffled blast from its engine, shot more steam into the air and began to move; and the platform, now almost empty except for officials and people waving goodbye, slipped out of sight. The train rumbled past railway yards, commercial buildings and empty concrete spaces. They passed through a rock cutting with slim trees on either side, and then the countryside opened up and they skirted the edge of a wide expanse of water. Night had almost fallen, but Keith could distinguish some large shapes like ships out there. He thought little of it and turned away from the window, taking Jeanne's latest letter out of his tunic pocket.

Loch Carrann
Monday, 5 April 1943

Dear Keith,

It is now a long time since I heard from you. I know it is not easy where you are, but please write soon and tell me how you are getting on.

LC is boring as ever. How I yearn for adventure!

No, seriously, we are all well and everyone sends their love. Janet is about to become an aunt. You remember Janet, don't you? Her sister went to live in London.

The potatoes are growing, the cows are producing their milk, the herrings are swimming. In other words, life is exactly the same as usual.

I take full advantage of the school library. I'm glad they still let me use it even though it's two years since I was a pupil there.

It was quarterly communion last week and folk came from far and near as usual. (Remember those quarterly communions!) We had a house full of people.

There is a ceilidh at Dingwall next month (not in LC, of course!!) and I hope Lizzie will agree to accompany me.

We are having calm weather at present.

Hoping this finds you in the best of spirits.

Beanacht leat,
Jeanne

He put the letter back in his pocket together with the brooch Jeanne had given him on his last leave, before he set sail for Egypt. She had recently finished school and had persuaded her mother to take her to Glasgow to stay with her older sister for a few days. Keith had caught the train to Glasgow so he could rendezvous with them at Bradfords Tea Room in Sauchiehall Street. Despite wartime rationing, the tea rooms offered a small choice of cakes and biscuits. He and Jeanne had deliberated carefully before choosing shortbread and a slice of pound cake. Jeanne still had the air of a schoolgirl, with puppy fat on her face and long, glossy hair.

When the moment arrived to say goodbye, she had said to Keith, "I've got something for ye. A wee minder. Something to remember us by while you're away." She reached into her skirt pocket and drew out a handkerchief lightly scented with lavender wrapped round a small object. "Open it in a wee while. Not now," she instructed. Then she gave him a soft kiss on the cheek. When he opened the gift later, he found it to be the Scottish thistle brooch that Jeanne sometimes wore to church. It was a reminder of where he came from and the girl he grew up with.

In the seat behind Keith, a boy and an older man were talking as they worked on a jigsaw puzzle.

"This is a stupid puzzle, Grandad. It doesn't fit together."

"Yes it does. You need to be patient. Let's search for the pieces with straight edges."

Ye need to be patient. Keith's father had said those words to him back in the village. He was thirteen, and his father had asked him to assist with work on the skiff he was building. Keith's task was to rub the wood with sandpaper, but he did this with bad grace.

I'm old enough to use the chisel. Why does Pa give me all the boring jobs?

"Sanding takes time," his father had said, "but it needs to be done. The wee tasks are important."

A cool breeze had sprung up, clouds scudded past and the water of the loch turned grey and choppy. Three local girls were out in a rowing boat: Lizzie, who was fifteen, and her younger sisters, Chrissie and Jeanne. Keith's father sniffed the air.

"It's time those girls headed back." He shouted at the girls but got no response. The breeze grew into a gale, and the girls' boat appeared to drift. "They're in trouble," his father said. "Come on!"

They sprinted to the water's edge, dragged a boat into the loch and clambered aboard. His father rowed out, manoeuvring the boat until it bobbed alongside the girls. "Climb across, Chrissie," he called out. "The lad will take yer place." Keith held the girls' boat fast while Chrissie, pale and frightened, struggled across. Then he scrambled aboard and seized the oars from

Lizzie, who looked exhausted, spent. Young Jeanne sat in the stern, her eyes bright with excitement. Keith drew strongly on the oars as the water slapped against the side of the boat. Each time he raised his head he saw Jeanne watching him. She never took her eyes off his face.

After they got the girls back to shore, Keith's father said to him, "Well done, laddie."

He beamed. Praise from his father was rare. And for the rest of the day he felt a quiet glow of satisfaction. He and his father had worked as a team, the only time he had ever recalled them doing so.

Keith began to doze, lulled by the rocking motion of the train. In his half-asleep, half-awake state another image swam into his mind, an even earlier image.

He was eleven years old. It was wintertime. They had finished their evening meal, one of his mother's warming mutton stews, and were still at the table, the four of them, his ma and pa, himself and Duncan. The room, which was living room and kitchen combined, was made cosy by the warm coal range.

His father cleared his throat and looked at his ma—his stern face always softened when his eyes were on her—and then at his brother and him. He said, "Yer maither and I have something we want to discuss wi' ye."

That made Keith feel important.

"I'm going to Inverness for three months. I have the chance of some extra work." He watched both boys as if to ensure they were listening. "Ye will help yer maither tend things here while I'm gone, won't ye?"

The boys both nodded, then the four of them discussed the specifics of what needed to be done over the next three months.

In later years, after Duncan's accident, after his mother grew ill and died, after he and his father grew apart, he used to think about that evening. He used to feel it, yearn for it. The four of them together, sitting around the table, secure in each other's company.

Keith opened his eyes and tried to look out the window, but all he saw was his own reflection and indistinguishable shapes flashing by. The time passed slowly. Occasionally the train shuddered to a halt with a roar of steam and the squeak of brake blocks, and people would get on or off. The grandfather and grandson disembarked at Moncton, New Brunswick. Then with more shuddering, hissing and roaring, the train began to move again.

The next thing Keith knew, Blue was shaking him awake. He must have curled up on his seat and dropped off to sleep. He screwed up his face with a groan as he gingerly stretched each cramped limb. It was morning, but the train still rattled along. The lights were on in the car and the air smelt stale.

Blue spoke to him in a low voice. "Are you carrying much cash on you?"

"Quite a lot. Why?"

"Well, listen. We're getting near the border, and the customs and immigration officials will come aboard. Remember, if they ask you any questions, we're just going to the first town across the other side to see some people, and we're only stopping there for twenty-four hours. Okay?"

Keith nodded and rubbed his eyes.

"Officially we're only allowed to take five Canadian dollars with us," Blue continued. "So hop along to the toilet and slip the rest into your sock. Put it right under the sole of your foot."

"What? Are they likely to search us?"

"No. Most of the customs officials are okay, but sometimes you get a zealous bastard."

Keith wriggled his feet into his shoes, then slowly straightened up. The seat had left aches and stiffness in more than one part of his body. He felt in his pocket for his wallet before making his way down the corridor towards the toilet, a little unsteady on his feet due to the motion of the train.

When the customs officers entered the car, Keith crossed one leg over the other so the shoe with the money in it was nearest the floor. As he pressed down, he was conscious of the bills against his foot. The official on his side of the car was the more severe of the two. He reprimanded someone whose papers were not in order. Keith had no paper beyond his identification card, and all the time those bills were sticking against his foot.

The official arrived in front of him, glancing first at the card and then at him. "Where were you born? Where are you going? How long for?"

Keith was nervous and his jaw felt stiff as he answered. However, before he knew it, the official had signed a twenty-four-hour chit and moved on. They were safely across. He slumped down into his seat, relieved. The train was already pulling up.

Blue and Stretch jumped to their feet.

Blue called across to Keith, "We'll get off here, have a meal, and then see what it's like on the road. With luck we'll strike plenty of traffic."

Half an hour later the three of them stood on the roadside near trees and open fields.

"Done much hitchhiking?" Blue asked.

"A little."

"Okay. Here are some tips. Never wait at the foot of a hill. Trucks going up won't stop. Never stop halfway down a hill. Cars going down won't stop. Watch the speed of the vehicles. It might be better to miss a slow truck and wait for a faster car. Apart from that, thumb everything that approaches. And the first question you ask them is, 'Where are you heading?'"

Chapter 6

Upstate New York
June 1943

Blue's optimism was not rewarded. Drivers did not seem keen to stop, and there were long waits between rides. It was disheartening, tiring.

By late afternoon, as they swung off a truck and waved goodbye to the driver, they were almost ready to call it a day. They spotted a tavern up the road and agreed that a sandwich and a beer would help them along.

They went inside and perched at the counter. A jukebox played in the corner, and the waiter placed glasses of iced water in front of them and tried to harmonise with the music. Stretch ordered sandwiches and a round of drinks, then stared moodily at his glass.

Keith tucked his feet in behind the stool, surveying the scene. The only other occupant of the bar sat just along from Blue. He wore a raincoat and a rakish hat that had slipped a little over one ear. An almost empty tumbler of what looked like Scotch sat in front of him. He grinned affably in their direction, and Blue grinned back.

"How's it going, mate?" Blue asked.

The stranger slid down on to his feet and made towards them. "This is good stuff, boys," he said, looking at each in turn as if expecting them to challenge his statement. He put an arm round Blue. "Here, let me get you some. Harry's the name."

He ordered drinks for them and they began talking. At least

Harry talked. Beyond an occasional word from Blue the others drank and listened.

Keith glanced at his watch. They still needed to find a place where they could park their gear and sleep. He swallowed some Scotch. It tore at his throat a little, but once it was down it was warm and good. They finished their first drink and Stretch ordered another round.

Their new friend was becoming enthusiastic. "Fellas, it's great to be with you. No fun drinking alone. Here's to a happy time." He raised his glass.

The drinks continued well into the night, with the men forming an easy camaraderie. Keith felt mellow and free from worry and forgot his tiredness.

"Did you hear the one about the Scotsman, the Englishman and the Australian?" Blue said. "They were having a few drinks, just like us, and had just started on a fresh round of beers when a fly landed in each glass. The Englishman lifted his out on the blade of his Swiss Army knife. The Australian blew his away. The Scotsman picked his up carefully by the wings, held it above his glass and said, 'Go on, spit it out, ye wee devil.'"

Keith peered into his glass. "No wee beasties there." He gestured at Stretch and quoted:

> *There was a young man of Australia*
> *Who painted his ass like a dahlia.*
> *The drawing was fine,*
> *The colour divine,*
> *The scent—ah, that was a failure.*

After that, they vied with each other to tell tall stories and jokes. Time and again the tavern filled with the laughter of the four men. Harry contributed his share of tales. In fact, there was little he did not reveal about himself.

"What about your wife?" Stretch asked. "When are you going to hit the trail for home?"

"That's all right, boys. Don't worry about it. I've been downstate with my work, and I'm not due home for a day or two yet. Where did you fellas say you were going? New York City, huh? You know, I've got half a mind to accompany you. Been a long time since I was there. Yes, sir, a long time. And it's a grand place, fellas. Believe me, it is."

Stretch's face brightened. "Listen, you've got an automobile outside, haven't you?"

"Yep, a 1940 Dodge Deluxe sedan."

"Well, what's keeping us?" Stretch continued. "How about giving us a lift? Come on, boys. Down the hatch and let's go, off to New York."

Harry voiced a feeble protest and Keith also hesitated, but only for a moment. The liquor had put them into that happy state of mind where it seemed that anything could be tackled. They shouted "Goodnight!" and piled out the doors to find the car.

When they had all clambered aboard, Harry started up the car and, with a loud "Yip!" from Stretch in the front seat alongside him, they were on their way.

The speedometer needle flicked up as they drove along. At first they sang. Raucous songs with little melody. Just as Keith was starting to doze off, there was a bump from one of the back tyres. At first they made fun of it, but then Harry pulled over and he and Stretch got out to investigate. They decided it would be all right for a while yet and drove on at a slower speed.

Keith was almost asleep again when he heard Stretch's voice.

"Hold her a minute, mate, and pull in by the side, will you."

A car was parked by the side of the road a short distance away, and they squeaked to a standstill beside it.

"Where do you keep your tools?" Stretch asked Harry.

"Under the front seat."

The four men stepped out on to the road, Keith rubbing his eyes.

Stretch took out the tools and jacked up the front wheel of the other car.

Harry looked puzzled. "What are you doing?"

Blue's hand dropped on to Harry's shoulder. "Don't panic. You've been a good friend, and we appreciate it. We'd like to do something for you in return." He squatted down to assist Stretch.

"But you can't do that!" protested Harry, as they started to remove a good tyre from the other car and swap it over. "It's someone else's property."

"Hell! Don't worry. You know nothing at all about it, okay? This is a little present from the boys. We'll leave a note of thanks if you like."

Keith watched Blue and Stretch work. They would get the job done more quickly without him contributing. He had never even travelled in a car until a few years ago, when he went to live with his widowed aunt in Edinburgh.

Mr McPhee, one of the elders from his aunt's church, used to take the two of them on occasional outings in his Austin Seven. One Saturday afternoon they did the Queensferry crossing to Fife. They drove to Kinghorn for afternoon tea and then motored around the area. On the return journey home in the early evening darkness, they got a puncture in one of the front tyres. Keith had hovered awkwardly while Mr McPhee fixed it. He remembered the Austin's headlights as being bright, whereas the headlights of this large American car were strangely dim. Something to do with battery power, perhaps, or his different perspective in time.

When Blue and Stretch had completed the changeover, the four of them climbed back into the car with Harry still protesting.

As they started up and pulled away, Stretch wiped his grimy hand on a rag, then half turned in his seat, waving in the direction of the parked car. "Thanks a lot for the help, mate," he called out. "We might get the chance to do the same for you one day."

Not long afterwards, Stretch motioned towards Harry, whose head had jerked forward several times as his eyes closed. "Time for some kip. And I need a piss. Let's pull off the road a bit."

Harry obediently pulled over. The men wandered away to relieve themselves. After returning to the car, they promptly buttoned up their coats, curled up as best they could and went to sleep.

Some hours later they woke. It was dawn, and the effects of the alcohol had subsided. Keith felt stiff and hungry, with feet like blocks of ice.

Beside him, Blue stretched out, making a wry face. "'Struth, what a mouth. Like the bottom of a birdcage."

There was a grunt from Stretch in the front seat. "Me too."

They agreed the best plan was to find somewhere to eat, and so they continued as far as a small town, where they parked the car in a side street.

Harry surveyed the new tyre with furrowed brow, then glanced around nervously as if expecting the rightful owner to appear at any moment.

Finding a cafe, they ordered coffee, hot cakes, bacon and eggs. They ate with gusto and when they had finished lit cigarettes and sat back, relaxing.

Harry stared at the table. "Sorry fellas, I got carried away last night. Much as I'd love to drive you to New York, it's time for me to head home."

"That's okay," Blue said. "We understand. You have other people to consider."

"I'll hit the road with you, if you don't mind," Keith said to Harry. "I don't want to get too far away from the ship—"

"Have we got a piker on our hands?" broke in Stretch. "I wouldn't have believed it of you." He looked at Blue. "So we're back to the old firm, just the two of us."

Blue nodded. "Seems like it." He turned to Keith. "We'll give you the address of our club in New York. Just in case."

As Keith and Harry drove off, they waved to the two Aussies standing by the doorway. "Well, there go two of the hardest customers I've ever met," Harry said.

Keith grinned. "I did hear once that most Aussies weren't born but quarried. They were good company, though. It's a pity that's the last we'll see of them."

Chapter 7

Halifax
June 1943

It was nearly six o'clock in the evening when Keith arrived back in Halifax. He made straight for the services canteen, as he needed a snack; and also he thought he might see Joe there. The haversack was still slung over his shoulder. He had not even opened it. For that matter, he had not removed his clothes since he left two days before; nor had he slept in a bed. But army life had accustomed him to dossing down wherever he found himself.

The canteen was almost deserted. No sign of Joe. He collected a meal, then moved across to a table and began devouring the generous serving of hot meat pie, potatoes and peas. After a while he became aware of the waitress clearing tables, the same girl whose trim figure Joe had admired the other day.

He called out to her, "Have you seen Joe anywhere?"

She frowned slightly as if she'd heard those lines before and shook her head. "I don't know anyone called Joe." She turned her back on him and continued her work.

Keith persisted. "You must have noticed Joe. He's a tall, strong chap with curly ginger hair. An Australian soldier. He came here with me two nights ago."

She swung around. "Oh yes. I remember him. He's gone. His ship left this morning."

Keith stared at her in disbelief. "The ship's gone?"

"Yes, hours ago."

There'll be no convoy ready yet, and the ship can't sail unescorted. How would she know anyway?

As if reading his thoughts, she added, "He came in last night looking for you. He told me the ship was leaving today."

The girl returned to her work, and Keith focused on his meal again, but it did not taste as good as it had a few minutes before. He had to force it bite by bite down his throat, which had suddenly become dry. He put down his fork.

What if she's right? I need to go to the pier and check for myself.

Keith managed to eat a few more mouthfuls, then he dropped his knife and fork on to his plate, rose quickly from the table and strode out of the canteen. He walked down Prince Street into Lower Water Street. Despite the nervous energy that carried him along, his steps slowed as he approached the pier. He wanted to delay the moment.

He rounded the side of a wharf building and came to a halt. Two khaki-clad men with distinctive MP brassards on their sleeves stood at the end of the pier. And there, almost directly in front of him, was his ship. The girl was wrong, thank God. He paused to regain his equilibrium. At that moment, there was a single loud cry, the voice of a man in pain, from somewhere nearby. The two military policemen began running in the direction of the noise. And then the pier and everything around him faded away into darkness. There was a deafening explosion, and someone calling his name. Jimmy.

Keith grasped the side of the building, unable to move, his head filled with pain. He had always looked out for Jimmy. But he had let Jimmy down.

Gradually his head cleared, and he realised he was still on the pier. Nothing in his surroundings had changed. But something inside him had. He knew one thing for sure.

I'm not going back. I can't be a soldier any more.

Sinking sank back into the shadows, he waited. Three sailors hurried along the pier and mounted the ship's gangway, pausing to have a word with the quartermaster, who stood at the top. Up on deck men secured moveable objects, tested the stanchions and handrails at the ship's side and checked lifeboats one by one. The boatswain appeared and moved around, inspecting the boats on their davits.

They're preparing to leave.

As though in a dream, Keith watched as the deck crew hoisted aboard the gangway and then cast off the mooring lines, one by one. At the stern, signalmen removed the ensign from the harbour ensign staff and replaced it with a smaller ensign at the aftermast. With a throbbing hum the turbines started up and, as the water whirled heavily under her stern, the ship slowly moved away from the pier.

Now what?

The pier was deserted.

I'll lie low in Halifax, simply disappear.

He turned his back on the departing ship and set off towards the town centre. In Barrington Street, he saw some military police on the other side of the road. They were talking to each other and did not glance his way, but the blood swirled in his head. The port was dangerous. Too many police. Better to move on, perhaps across the border.

That's it. I'll make for New York. It'll be easier to hide there, and I'll have company too. Blue and Stretch. I'll take the train tonight.

Chapter 8

Keith sat nervously in the train as it pulled away from Halifax station and began rattling along the route he had travelled three days previously, through the rock cutting and around the edge of the huge expanse of water. Again he saw ships there, lying low in the water, and he suddenly realised why. He started violently, his heart racing.

That's the Bedford Basin. They're loaded with cargo, waiting for a convoy to form. Our ship will be there.

The man seated beside him gave him a curious look, and Keith gripped the edge of his seat to stop himself from leaping to his feet. He tried to control his breathing.

They'll realise I'm gone, but Joe will have made up some story, that I haven't recovered from my concussion, that I went missing on the voyage. Anyway, I'll soon be well away from here. It's not my ship any more.

Gradually the steady rhythm of the train soothed him.

To his surprise, Keith encountered no problems at the border. He used the same story as previously, and the official, a friendly one this time, gave him a twenty-four-hour chit. He left the train at the first town on the other side, soon landing a long lift with a truck driver. This was followed by a series of shorter lifts, the last of which left him on Highway 9 on the east side of the Hudson River.

His run of luck continued when a cream coupe drew up almost immediately. The driver, who introduced himself as Walter Simon, was slim-faced with thick-lensed glasses; and, although he looked to be still in his twenties, his fair hair was thinning on top.

As they accelerated away, Walter glanced across at Keith's balmoral. "No need to ask where you hail from. Where in Scotland exactly?"

"A village in the Western Highlands."

Walter gave him a quick look, head on one side.

Keith added, "Lochcarron, or *Loch Carrann*, as we say in the Gaelic. It's on a huge loch, an arm of the sea."

"I'd like to explore Scotland someday. Has your family been there long?"

"Generations. I come from a long line of crofters."

Walter had a friendly, alert manner and Keith lowered his guard a little. He explained that he had also lived in Edinburgh for a while, and in other parts of Scotland during his army training, and had later served in Egypt. Then, not wishing to talk more about himself, he asked, "What about you? Do you live locally?"

"Brooklyn. I've been upstate visiting my parents. They still live in the town where I grew up. My father practises medicine there."

"Are you in the medical field too?"

Walter gave a short laugh. "No, we've got enough medics in the family. I much prefer investigating people and issues."

Keith's mouth was suddenly dry. His hand reached for the door handle and then he withdrew it again when he saw how much it was shaking. He felt his facing burning.

Walter glanced at Keith but said nothing for a few minutes. Then he began speaking, slowly. "I studied journalism at Columbia and now I'm a reporter for the *Brooklyn Daily Eagle*." He paused. "Are you all right, Keith? You look as if you've had some sort of attack."

Keith's heart was thumping and there was a roaring in his head. But he knew he had to say something. He took a deep breath. "I get jumpy sometimes. Don't know why."

Walter looked at him again, and then he spoke in a calm voice. "I failed the medical for military service, so now my ambition is to become a war correspondent based in London. I speak French and German. Before the war I spent a year at a university in Berlin. My grandparents came from there. And I'm hoping that will help." He stopped talking, and gestured to the right. "That's Hyde Park, the home of our president, Franklin D. Roosevelt."

Walter slowed the car, and Keith looked across at a mansion with columned porticos in a park-like estate.

The steady motion of the car made Keith feel drowsy. Later Walter drew his attention to West Point, the United States Military Academy, high on the western bank of the river, and explained a little of its history.

"This is also the land of 'Rip Van Winkle.' The towns have names like Catskill, Fishkill and Peepskill."

Keith sat up in his seat. "I know about 'Rip Van Winkle.'"

"Ha. That roused you, didn't it?" Walter said. "You look as if you're short of sleep."

"Aye, but let's not talk about that. Try getting your tongue around *Achnashellach* instead."

Walter grinned. "I think I'll take a rain check. If I try saying that right now, we'll probably swerve off the road."

He continued to point out features along the way, and they even took a short detour from the highway to see the grim walls of Sing Sing Prison beside the river.

Keith found Walter's enthusiasm infectious. "These places were just names to me before," he said.

"What about the people?" Walter asked.

"The people who live round here?" Keith shook his head. "The only Americans I've met are the ones who've been kind enough to give me lifts."

"There's an amazing mix of people living down this eastern bank, mixed together or in separate settlements. Poles and Greeks, Italians and Germans, Dutch and Jews and Irish, all now swearing allegiance to the one flag."

"Well. I had no idea. To tell the truth, I know very little about America. You must think me narrow and ignorant," he added, "knowing so little about other countries and other peoples."

Walter laughed. "Not at all. That's the kind of thing other countries sometimes accuse Americans of—inward-looking and so on."

Keith laughed too. He thought for a moment and then said, "I know a lot about Scottish history, but I also learned about European history. That was the year I lived with my aunt in Edinburgh. She paid for me to go to a posh school. I hated it at first, had nothing in common with the other boys. But they accepted me after they found I was good at sport."

"You're lucky. I was never any good at sport. I was just brainy," Walter said. "What kind of things did you learn about European history?"

"France mostly. There was an Auld Alliance between the kingdoms of Scotland and France. It was drawn up by John Balliol and Philip IV."

"I like history," Walter said. He glanced across at Keith. "If it wasn't for the fact that you boys prefer to enjoy the hospitality in Manhattan, I'd give you a firm invitation to come and see me at the *Brooklyn Eagle*. I'd take you out for a drink. The general invitation's there, anyway. You'll have no trouble finding where our office is. The servicemen's desk will give you directions."

"Thanks," Keith said. "I might do that."

Walter glanced across at him. "I'm curious about people, it's true. But you needn't worry that I'd try to unravel your deepest secrets."

For a moment Keith was tempted to tell Walter the truth about himself. But he suppressed the thought.

They were closer to the river now. Walter explained that the high-cliffed shore on the other side was New Jersey and they were already in Yonkers and the outskirts of New York City. They came to a toll bridge, crossed to Manhattan and continued along the Henry Hudson Parkway. Keith leaned forward in awe. On one side was the river, spanned by a giant bridge; on the other were blocks of apartment buildings, taller than he had ever seen before. Not just a single block, but block after block.

Further up the river there had been merchantmen, heavily laden with cargo lashed to their decks; now there were ocean-going liners. Walter drove deeper into the maze of piers and buildings and the ramps and roadways that served them. They had left the expressway and were down below in the bustling life of the port itself. Keith looked from side to side, unwilling to miss anything. Then Walter turned away from the piers, into the labyrinth of the city. Keith's head spun as he tried to follow their route. There was too much detail and too many people, and it all blurred into the evening shadows that clothed the streets.

"I'll drop you off in Park Avenue, just short of the Grand Central terminal," Walter said. "There's a bureau in the main concourse, and they'll be able to arrange a place to stay for you."

Keith felt almost regretful when they reached their destination. He was about to say goodbye to a new friend whom he might never see again. But he got out promptly and thrust his hand across to Walter. "Thank you for the lift, and the conversation. You've whetted my appetite for New York."

"The pleasure was mine. Enjoy the city," Walter said. "Once you reach the terminal you'll see some swinging doors. Go through those and then it's not far to the main concourse." With a wave of his hand he drove off.

Keith watched him turn the corner, then pulled his haversack higher on his shoulder and walked towards the Grand Central terminal.

He stepped through the swinging doors into the hurly-burly of the huge terminus. All around him, people entered through numerous doors and hurried by. In the space of a few seconds, a middle-aged man in a business suit and trilby hat, a young woman wearing a pretty coat and high heels that tapped on the marble floor, an older woman holding firmly on to the hands of two children, and a group of soldiers with kitbags slung over their shoulders all walked past. He stopped in his tracks, overwhelmed, his heart drumming in his chest. There were so many people, so much bustle, and he was not part of it.

He shook his head in an attempt to clear it. Then he let himself be swept along in the stream of people that flowed down the gentle slope to the grand vestibule with its towering vaulted ceilings. Pale shafts of light filtered in through three tall windows, which were curved at the top and made up of narrow lead-rimmed panes. He paused for a moment to get his bearings, then pressed on through the crowd and joined the queue waiting at the services information desk. He was tired, almost swaying on his feet, and his mind drifted away.

He was waiting in line at the Inverness Railway Station ticket office, with his father standing beside him. He shifted his head slightly to look at his father. He had something he wanted to say to him. But his father stared straight ahead, rigid and preoccupied. Even though they stood shoulder to shoulder, an abyss gaped between them.

Eventually his father said, "Ye'll be guid for your aunty, won't you? Won't give her trouble?"

Keith mumbled a response.

"Ye can come home for Christmas and see yer friends."

He shrugged his shoulders and said nothing.

"What can we do for you, son?" The voice was friendly.

Keith gave a start. He had reached the front of the line and the woman at the desk had addressed him. "Sorry," he said. "I want accommodation for several days. Something easy on the pocketbook."

The woman directed him to an inexpensive hotel and, as he prepared to walk away, added, "Good luck. And remember about the buses. If you're rolling in money, you can ride the bus on Fifth Avenue for a dime, but if you go down a block either way you can get there just as fast for a nickel."

Keith grinned as he felt in his pocket. There was no need to worry about that yet.

When he had showered and cleaned up, he went searching for Blue and Stretch at the ANZAC Club in West 56th Street. They were not there, but the woman at the desk knew them well.

"Try the Hotel Astor in Times Square. You can't miss the Astor. It's spread over a whole block. Go into the bar. If the liquor hasn't run out, you'll probably find those two holding the floor."

Chapter 9

New York City
June 1943

The lounge bar of the Hotel Astor was crowded. All the chairs and tables were occupied and people lined both sides of the long oval bar. There was a loud babble of conversation interspersed with periodic bursts of laughter. Everyone seemed to be firmly established, leaving no window for a stranger to break into their group.

Keith scanned the room and was relieved to spot the boys seated around a table with several others. He stood for a moment watching them, then moved in their direction. Blue had the floor, while Stretch stared at his glass. He had probably heard Blue's story numerous times before.

Blue paused, gazing around as if to gauge the effect he was having on his audience. He suddenly noticed Keith and broke into a broad grin. "Well, look what the wind's blown in!"

Stretch raised his head, yawning, and gaped at Keith. "How's my old mate? Come and join the happy gang."

He introduced Keith to the group and someone pulled a chair for him from a neighbouring table.

"What's it going to be, sport?" Blue asked.

"I've just got in," Keith said, "and I'm feeling weary. Two drinks, and then I'm off to hit the pit."

Blue assumed an expression of grief. "Bed? Tonight? Forget it, son. We'll take care of you."

After two drinks Keith was still at the table, and the group grew larger and merrier. A New Zealand airman wandered in, heading towards the bar, and Blue called out. "Come and join us, sport."

The newcomer, a big, loose-limbed fellow, sat down with a friendly nod to the men opposite him. He introduced himself as Dave.

One of the Americans, an older man, enquired, "Say, this Noo Zealand. Where is it?"

"That's the idea, mate," Blue said. "New Zealand's a few little islands twelve hundred miles east of Australia. You have trouble locating them when the tide's in. One of these days there'll be a decent wave and they'll disappear altogether."

Dave roared with mirth, his whole body shaking. "Don't listen to him. He's *je-a-lous*." His voice was booming, resonant. "New Zealand is an oasis in the South Pacific, to the east of a desert they call Australia."

The American looked puzzled. "You're not a native of Noo Zealand, are you? Your English is very good."

"Ah yes." Dave had a nostalgic expression on his face. "The mission schools. I owe them a debt of gratitude."

"You don't say! Those missions do good work."

Blue, who had been temporarily overshadowed by Dave, regained his voice. "Hard to believe that a few generations ago his ancestors were cannibals, isn't it?"

Keith was amused that Blue had switched from baiting the New Zealander, to uniting with him to have on the American. Their two countries obviously had a love-hate relationship like England and Scotland.

Now Stretch joined in too. "It's the same back home in Aussie. I've come across the bones of many an American missionary lying bleached in the sun. It's mostly been bred out of us, but every now and then the cannibal streak breaks out."

The group erupted into laughter.

The American studied the amused faces and then, realising they were having a joke at his expense, joined in good-humouredly. "Okay boys, you got me there. Next round's on me."

Leaving the bar several hours later, Keith wandered the streets in a happy mood. He discovered New York to be a city that did not sleep. The theatres on Broadway were still open at midnight, the hotel bars until two in the morning and the nightclubs until after three. At four o'clock he went into an eating house for a hamburger and a cup of coffee. He sat in the window and watched as the stragglers from the night made their way home.

Soon afterwards the shutters started going up; the day was taking over. Under the glare of a streetlight, a newspaper vendor laid out the early edition of a morning paper. A man stopped to buy one, opening it up immediately, and Keith strained to see the headline: Allies bomb Sicily and Italian mainland. Then he averted his gaze. The war was not his concern any more.

He drained the last of his coffee and climbed down off the stool. The man behind the counter collected the plate and cup, wiped the table and ambled back to his post, glancing up at the clock.

Keith buttoned his tunic a little higher and, with a cheery "so long", set off walking to his hotel. He kicked at a tin can that lay on the pavement. It pinged and shot off at an angle on to the road. He chuckled to himself.

It was almost noon when he woke up. After taking a shower he went out to explore, across the streetcar lines, under the elevated railway on Third Avenue, and deep into the maze of steel and concrete at the heart of the metropolis. The images in his head from the night before were of crowded streets and brightly coloured lights. But it was different by day. None of the cities he knew—Edinburgh, Birmingham, London, Cairo—had prepared him for these buildings. They towered above him and even at midday cast long shadows on the streets. He marvelled at the modernity of it all.

Over the next few days, he spent time with Blue and Stretch and made the most of what New York had to offer. He lined up for cheap tickets to Broadway theatres, took ferry rides, and climbed the twisting steps inside the Statue of Liberty. With his uniform as a passport he dined and drank at exclusive clubs along with other guests in uniform. He deliberately suppressed thoughts of his previous life. Only once did he think about Walter Simon's offer, and he was too busy to follow it up.

One day, walking down Park Avenue on his way to meet Blue and Stretch, he came across several people walking dogs. Dogs of all shapes and sizes, it seemed, would stop every now and then at one of the patches of earth spaced along the footpath. He paused to contemplate two elaborately clipped toy poodles tripping past and immediately thought of Joe.

What would he have to say about these pampered creatures?

Thinking of Joe unsettled Keith and he suddenly felt displaced. The people around him were busy living their own lives and all had somewhere to go. The taxicabs—green, yellow, red—that raced in and out of the traffic accentuated this.

Half an hour later, in the jovial company of Blue and Stretch, he put sombre thoughts out of his mind.

One morning Blue and Stretch did not turn up at the usual meeting place. Keith waited for a while and then, suspecting they had overslept, made his way to their room. He found them hastily packing. Even Stretch moved fast.

"Sorry, mate. It's goodbye," Blue said, as he whirled around the room hurling items of clothing into his kitbag. "The grapevine warning has just arrived—late. We need to return to camp. Our posting's due in a few days."

Keith was stunned. They were about to rejoin their unit; he was not.

By eleven o'clock the two Australians were on the road bound for Canada. Keith, for want of a better plan, accompanied them. They were picked up on the open highway by a truck driver, and Keith travelled with them as far as Albany, New York. He had decided he would go to Montreal from there.

As the truck drew up on the roadside, the driver pointed out a canteen where he could get hot coffee, something to eat, and perhaps a bed for the night. Keith jumped down on to the side of the road, then stretched up to clasp the hand of each Australian in turn. They wished him luck, and as the truck pulled away he stood on the footpath and watched them disappear. From now on he would face life in a strange land by himself, without Blue and Stretch's confidence and cheek as a shield. The wind cut through him, so he turned quickly, hitching his bag over his shoulder, and walked towards the door of the canteen.

There were not many people inside but it looked warm and inviting. Two men played billiards near the door. Further in there were easy chairs and a table covered in magazines and books. Music wafted from a radio near the wall. At the far end of the room there was a coffee urn, and a counter behind which a woman was preparing a sandwich. Keith climbed on to a stool and watched her.

She looked up, smiling, and moved over to him wiping her hands on her apron. "You look like you've had a long day. How does some coffee sound?"

She had a friendly, open manner and Keith began to relax.

"Just what I need," he said.

The coffee was strong and hot, the sandwich well filled, and the lemon pie sweet and satisfying. While he ate, he broached the subject of a bed for the night.

The woman was apologetic. "I'm afraid the canteen is non-residential and I don't know of any servicemen's accommodation in town."

Keith had not expected this. He frowned as he tried to think what he should do now.

"Would you like me to arrange an introduction to a private home for you?" she asked. "We have a number of people who are willing to have you boys as guests."

Keith paused. He would feel awkward in a strange household. But then again, he did not have many options.

The woman looked expectant. "Is the answer yes?"

He nodded. "Thank you."

Chapter 10

Albany, New York
July 1943

There was only one light in the street, and the houses were set back slightly from the footpath, so the numbers were hard to see. Keith resorted to counting the houses until he found the right one. He pressed the doorbell and had scarcely released his finger when the door opened and an interior light flashed on.

Taken aback, he began to stammer his introduction to the woman standing before him. "Um, I …"

She quickly came to his assistance. "Keith?"

"Yes, the canteen—"

"I'm Mrs Spaulding. We're expecting you. Come in."

Keith followed her inside, shutting the door behind him.

He saw her more clearly now. She was of medium height with strong features, friendly eyes and dark brown hair that was closely cut for a woman.

She led him into the living room. "I believe you've had a long day on the road."

Keith waited for a moment. He must be careful what he said. "Yes, it's been quite a hard day."

She had a quick, decisive manner. "Did you travel from New York this afternoon?"

Again, Keith paused.

Before he could answer, she said, "But here I am talking away, and you're probably famished. Would you like a bite to eat?"

"Well, as a matter of fact, I've already eaten at the canteen."

"But you would eat something if I cooked it for you, wouldn't you? It won't take long, and then you won't need to worry about getting up so early in the morning, especially if you're in no hurry to get back on the road." Keith detected both kindness and firmness in her tone. "There's fruit juice here, and how about some breakfast?" she continued.

Keith abandoned any attempt at argument. "Now you mention it, I do feel a bit hungry."

"Good. Come and sit down and relax. It'll be ready for you in no time."

Keith followed her into the kitchen. Leaning with one elbow on the steel-topped bench, he watched her as she worked over the stove. He glanced around him. There was a white refrigerator in the corner and a table accompanied by a bench seat along each side, set compactly in a recess. He felt warm and comfortable, and his mouth began watering at the crisp splutter and smell of bacon frying in an open pan. His mind drifted back to the house he grew up in, and the small combined living room and kitchen with its coal range and paraffin lamp. He smiled to himself. They had used that room for everything. They had bathed in it and even slept there at times when there were visitors. What would his mother have made of this clean, modern American kitchen?

He was seated at the table with bacon and eggs, hot coffee and warm buttered rolls before him, when the back door opened and Mr Spaulding came in. He was a tall man, heavily built, with fair hair receding on either side of his forehead. His handshake was firm and Keith warmed to him instantly.

"By the way," the woman said. "We're happy for you to call us Vi and Art. 'Mr and Mrs Spaulding' is rather formal and stiff, and 'Mom and Pop' makes us feel old. But call us whatever you feel comfortable with."

Art sat down opposite Keith. "When do you have to return to your base?" he asked.

Keith finished his mouthful of food and took a moment before answering. "Not for a while yet. I'm hitching my way back, making it by easy stages."

"Well, why not stay with us a little longer? You're most welcome."

"That would be much more pleasant than getting back to camp too early," Keith said.

"Good. We'll be only too glad to have you."

Afterwards Keith had a bath, almost the first since he joined the service. For nearly an hour he lay there, relaxed, cocooned. Now and then he sat up and reached forward lazily to add more hot water.

It was late when he retired to his room. He laid his hand on the bed. It was soft and generous-sized and had a lamp conveniently above it. There was also a bedside table with a plate of fresh fruit, a dish of candy, a portable radio, and the latest *Reader's Digest*. Like the rest of the house the room was cool from the air conditioning.

So this is an American home, Keith thought. He smiled contentedly and stretched out on his back.

"It's good to have a guest who's meticulous about his appearance," Vi said to Keith next morning. "And who bothers to bathe and wash out socks and underwear." She gave a wry smile. "Last week we had two young fellas who climbed into bed every night without the benefit of soap or water. On the rare occasions they ventured into the bathroom, they'd leave the door open. I felt guilty when Art suggested I send them on their way, but I was relieved too."

One night soon extended to a week. Keith's reserve broke down and he fitted with ease into the household. Vi and Art both worked, she as a hospital pharmacist and he as a railway engineer, and they gave Keith a key so he could come and go freely. He walked Vi's dog, a Maltese terrier, and sometimes the neighbour's dog too. When he mentioned that he enjoyed reading and was interested in learning about America, Vi handed him *The Last of the Mohicans* by James Fennimore Cooper.

"This author lived most of his life in Cooperstown, New

York, about sixty miles from here. You'll enjoy the book," she said.

"I remember reading it as a child."

She looked surprised. "It's interesting you should have read that story back in Scotland, because it's set near here. The Indians were a tribe from this state. If it ever did happen, it happened around here."

"Vi knows a lot about America for a foreigner," Art said.

"Foreigner?"

"Don't listen to him," Vi said. "He likes to tease me about the fact that I was born in Canada. My parents lived there for several years. They returned to New York when I was three years old."

Over the next few days, Keith worked his way through Vi and Art's library of books on the history of America, tracing the locations on a large-scale map of the eastern states that Art brought home for him. Vi and Art also subscribed to magazines—*Life*, *National Geographic*, *Scientific American*, *Ladies Home Journal* and *American Engineer and Railroad Journal*—and he often dipped into them after supper.

One evening he commented to Art, "When I first arrived in America and I heard Americans boasting about their country it irritated me a bit. I thought they were full of hot air, or perhaps there was a national inferiority complex."

"So you've decided that's not the full picture?"

"Aye. I still marvel at how modern and efficient everything is. And it's a land of opportunity, isn't it? If you work hard, you improve your situation in life. Not like back home. In New York I found people accepted me because of my uniform, not because of my breeding or rank."

Art's eyes were amused. "You'll give us swelled heads. But seriously, it's not all milk and honey here. Sure, New York is a great city, and she has the welcoming arms of the Statue of Liberty at her gates. But she's got her prejudices too. If your face were black, for instance, you wouldn't have so many opportunities. You might be able to achieve what you wanted, but only if you knew your place, and that means entering through the tradesmen's entrance and never knocking on the front door. And you'd even notice efforts to confine you to certain sections of the city."

"That's not to say we aren't proud of our country," Vi said, entering the conversation with some emphasis. "But it's still a work in progress. Anyway, tell us more about Scotland."

Keith raised his fist in the air and began singing:

> *Scots, wha hae wi' Wallace bled,*
> *Scots, wham Bruce has aften led,*
> *Welcome to your gory bed.*
> *Or to victorie!*

Vi and Art applauded, and he sang the song to the end:

> *Lay the proud usurpers low!*
> *Tyrants fall in every foe!*
> *Liberty's in every blow!*
> *Let us do, or dee!*

"That's a battle cry," Vi said.

"Aye, it's by Robbie Burns, and it's about the Battle of Bannockburn, the decisive battle of our first War of Independence." He talked to them at length about King Robert the Bruce and his army being outnumbered three to one, and the Scottish victory over the English after two bloody days of fighting.

"I did a coach tour in Scotland when I was a young man," Art said. "We were driving through the countryside when the driver pointed out, 'Over there is where the Scottish pulverised the English.' A little further on, he said, 'This is the place where the Scottish massacred the English.' Not far down the road he pointed to the right: 'Here was the battlefield where the Scottish whipped the English.' At that point, one of the other passengers said in a stiff English accent, 'My good man, didn't the English win any battles around here?' 'Not when I'm driving the bus,' was the response."

Keith laughed. "I was getting a bit carried away, wasn't I? But let me tell you one more story about Scotland. It's not a long one, I promise you." His voice took on a serious tone. "There was a tradition in one of the villages that when a baby boy was born, a tappit hen of malt whisky was put down to be drunk on his twenty-first birthday or his wedding day, whichever occurred first."

Vi looked puzzled, and so he explained, "By tappit hen, I mean a wee barrel. Anyway, one of the old men of the village, Andra, lay dying, and his lifelong friend Hamish came to visit him. When it was time for Hamish to leave, Andra said, 'I'm glad ye came tae see me because there's a favour I want tae ask. Ye ken that tappit o' whisky that was put doon at my birth? Well, I spent my twenty-first birthday on Flanders Field, and as ye ken, I never married, so what I wuid like ye tae do is pour it o'er my grave.' Tears streaming from his eyes, Hamish said, 'Aye, my friend, I'll do that for ye.' He walked to the door, and then turned and gave a lingering look at Andra. 'That wee barrel o' whisky I'm going to pour o'er yer grave. Would ye mind awfully much if it passed through my kidneys first?'"

There was a moment's silence, then Art chuckled. "I can't offer you a barrel o' whisky. I'll go back a gallon of stiff coffee instead."

Art loaned Keith some civilian clothes: shirt, trousers, and shoes that were well worn but proved a good fit for him. He enjoyed being out of uniform for a change, and during the day he relaxed. However, it was a different story at night.

When he finally fell asleep, he would have a terrible dream. There were cries of wounded and dying men; there was darkness and pain and confusion. Yet somehow he was not with the other men, where he should have been, but floated at a safe distance above them. Jimmy was down there, with Sergeant MacFarlane and Mack. They were falling into danger and only Keith saw it coming. He had to save them! He reached out to grip them, but they kept slipping away from his grasp. Every time he pulled one man to safety, another slid away. Then the ground beneath them crumbled, and he began floating away from them.

He would wake up in a cold sweat. He would tell himself there was nothing he could have done to help the others, but it made no difference.

During his waking hours he rarely thought of the explosion; but when night came, he had the nightmare all over again. He grew to dread the darkness of night, so he read in bed until late and then left the light on, draping his shirt over it.

One evening, he and Vi sat chatting in the nook by the fireplace. As usual, she had something in her hands. This time it was a one of the vests she was knitting for soldiers overseas.

She finished her row and said, "There's something I've been meaning to say to you." She paused. "I don't want to appear mean, but we don't leave lights on unnecessarily. Maybe you read so late that you fall asleep over your book?" She smiled at him.

Keith pondered for a moment. Perhaps he should tell her the whole story? Right now. But what would that achieve? It might be a relief for him, but it would implicate Vi. He decided to tell her part of the truth. "When I was in North Africa our Bren Carrier ran over a landmine. The others were all killed. I was wounded and suffered concussion. I have nightmares about it. The doctor told me that rest was the only thing that would cure it." He was careful to look at Vi as he prepared to lie to her. "My term in Canada is regarded mainly as a convalescent period. They're also using me as an instructor for recruits who are yet to see overseas action."

He wondered how convincing his explanation was, and he hoped Vi would not question him about his duties as an instructor. But she simply said, "Yes. Recovering from a serious concussion takes time."

"I'll make sure I turn off the light tonight," he said.

"No." She leaned over and touched his arm. "Now I know the reason, I'm not at all worried about that. Keep it on as long as you need it. I understand."

One day he took his uniform into town to have it pressed. When he returned, Vi had a visitor: Mrs Stuart, a Scottish lady who had immigrated to America many years before. She was an imposing-looking woman with tightly permed grey hair.

"I thought you might like to chat with someone about home," Vi said.

Keith felt wary. He would enjoy talking to a fellow Scot, but Mrs Stuart had a sharp gaze, as if she would not miss a thing. However, once the two of them started talking about Scotland he forgot his reservations. He became more and more animated, and Vi looked on, smiling.

At the end of his stay, when Keith said his farewells, Vi and Art pressed him to return as soon as he had more leave. He made for the outskirts of town and waited just past an intersection, thumbing all vehicles that were going south, as he had decided that his best option was to return to New York. It was not long before a large truck drew on to the side of the road near him. At the same moment, a car going in the opposite direction slowed down with its horn tooting, and someone called out and waved an arm. He waved in return and climbed on to the truck. This was a much better option: the car was heading the wrong way for him.

Chapter 11

New York City
July 1943

Back in New York, Keith avoided returning to the places he had patronised with Blue and Stretch. People would recognise him and wonder why he had so much spare time. Instead he concentrated on finding new places to go, new ways to survive while eking out his funds.

He quickly learned that a serviceman who knew the ropes could live very cheaply. There were clubs that provided a free meal, a meal that satisfied; others that offered a bed, either free or for a small payment. Uptown there was a Jewish USO, a large friendly, club; and there was a Catholic canteen just off Fifth Avenue under the giant shadow of St. Patrick's Cathedral. There was also the Presbyterian church, where he could attend Sunday morning service and go home to dinner afterwards as a guest of one of the congregation. In numerous other clubs and canteens he could get a snack and a drink or an offer of hospitality in a private home for a few days. He became acquainted with them all, but he was also aware of the need for caution: sometimes passes or identity cards had to be shown, or books signed. He spaced his visits to prevent himself from becoming too well known, and he varied his habits and routines to avoid frequenting the same part of town too often.

Keith's sleep was restless and disturbed because of his recurring nightmare, so he was always tired. On several occasions during the day, he experienced flashbacks about the explosion, triggered by the loud cry of a man in pain. No one but himself knew of these episodes, until one afternoon in the Lower East Side.

He was walking past the entrance to an alleyway when he suddenly stopped short. From within the narrow passageway came a sharp yelping that went on and on. There was a roaring in his head, and then he began running in the direction of the sound. This time he was going to save Jimmy. It was as if darkness had suddenly fallen, but he could dimly make out a man kicking a crying dog.

He felt himself gripping his hands round the man's throat.

Strong arms hauled him off the man he had been about to throttle. "You'll kill him!"

As his head cleared, he stared, confused, at the man towering over him. It was a British soldier, accompanied by two others.

"We noticed your uniform," the man said, "and saw you acting odd and heard the commotion, so we followed up. Just as well. Do you want to end up in the nick?"

Keith shook his head, still dazed.

"Been through some tough times?"

"Aye."

The dog had disappeared, and the man who had been ill-treating it slunk away too. The soldiers escorted Keith back to the main thoroughfare, offering to buy him a drink, but he declined. He was in no mood to talk to anyone right now. It frightened him that he had been so out of control.

In the evening he returned to his small room, which he kept meticulously, compulsively tidy—his one way of imposing order on his life. He removed his boots and lined them up neatly beneath the bed, which he had made that morning with the sheets smooth and taut, the corners immaculate. After he had done his ablutions, he lifted the mattress and spread his uniform underneath to press it. Then he lay down on his back, just as he did every night.

From time to time Keith saw newspaper headlines: ALLIES INVADE SICILY ... MUSSOLINI FALLS ... END OF SICILY CAMPAIGN ... BRITISH TROOPS INVADE ITALY. Sometimes he imagined his platoon there, purposeful and involved, but then he would suppress the thought.

One day in mid-September, he was gazing abstractedly into the window of a department store when he heard a voice at his elbow.

"You look as if you've got a load of worries on your shoulders."

A young woman of about his own age stood beside him. Her hair was light brown, rolled slightly at the front, and fell into soft curls almost to her shoulders. She was smartly dressed in a neat skirt and jacket, and heels that were high enough to show off her trim ankles.

"A little fed up, I suppose," Keith said.

"Fed up? In New York? Folk who live here might tire of the place, but not a visitor, surely."

"New York is amazing, but it can get lonely."

She studied him for a moment before speaking again. "Listen, I'm doing some shopping. It's my father's birthday soon, and I don't know what to buy him. You can help me pick something out, if you like." Her voice was encouraging.

He accepted the offer instantly. "Yes. I'll help you."

She extended her hand. "By the way, I'm Barbara Walker."

Keith introduced himself, then moved to the outside of the footpath and they set off together. It felt good to have company.

They went in and out of shops, trying on gloves, viewing socks, sniffing men's colognes and comparing the patterns on ties. Barbara seemed oblivious to the fact that he had been a total stranger a short while before.

"I've made up my mind," she said, holding up a tie. It was rust brown, with woven birds in black with a touch of blue.

"Are you quite sure now?"

She laughed. "Yes. I couldn't have done it without you."

She got the tie gift-wrapped, and by the time they emerged on to the street, the crowds were thick; it was lunchtime. They turned a corner on to a slightly quieter street, then paused with their backs to an office building. Keith pointed out a photographer on the other side of the road. He had his camera to his eye, ready to snap a soldier and his girl who were strolling towards him with their arms entwined.

"A street photographer," Barbara said. "Most of them do a good job, but there are occasional bad eggs who'll take your money and address, but the photo never arrives. It's the same in any big city, I guess."

From nearby a clock started to strike and Barbara gave a start. "It's time I got back to work."

"I'll walk you there."

"There's no need; it's just up the road."

"What do you do?"

"I'm a stenographer." She paused. "What are your plans for this afternoon?"

He glanced up at the sky. The sun shone in a large clear patch immediately above. "I'll make the most of this warmth and find somewhere to sunbathe."

Barbara touched his arm. "Why don't you spend the afternoon in Central Park? There are plenty of spots to lie in the sun, and if you like, I'll meet you there after work. I finish at five. We can take a stroll around the park and then catch the subway back to my apartment and have supper. What do you think?"

Keith hesitated. Joe would have jumped at the opportunity, but to him it was strange to be going to the apartment of a girl he had only just met. On the other hand, he and Barbara seemed to have quickly fallen into an easy friendship.

"Well?" She looked at him quizzically. "Would it help you decide if I mentioned there's chicken and homemade butterscotch pie? It's too much for me to eat. I'd appreciate having someone to share it with."

"All right," he said. "I'd like that."

"I'll meet you shortly after five at the Bethesda Fountain. It has an angel on top." She turned and walked away, entering a building further up the street.

Keith lounged on one of the wooden benches in Central Park, watching the people walking past. A woman approached, accompanied by a young man. He would have been in his twenties; she was much older, in her late forties perhaps, and was full-figured, with dark hair and olive skin. As she drew near, he had the feeling he had met her before, and he searched his memory. It was only when she glanced across at him that he suddenly worked it out: she reminded him of Samia, the woman in the Cairo brothel. How simple his life had been then.

He continued sitting there, enjoying the sun on his face, until he realised his head was beginning to nod. He saw there was a large lawn nearby where a sprinkling of people lay sunning themselves, so he wandered over and settled himself on the grass. An hour or two later he woke with a start and set off immediately for the Bethesda Fountain.

He arrived to see Barbara approaching from the opposite direction.

She smiled and said, "Perfect timing."

Early evening in Central Park was very pleasant. Some of the trees were already beginning to change colour and their leaves were scattered over the grass. The last shafts of sunlight streamed through gaps in the skyline between buildings that stood out in stark relief. Children fed pigeons, their excited chatter mingling with the cooing of the birds. Occasionally there was the clip-clop of horses' hooves and an old-fashioned Victoria carriage came into view, the driver up front with eyes only for his horses, and the couple behind with eyes only for each other.

Keith and Barbara strolled for some time, their arms lightly linked. A squirrel appeared on the grass in front of them and watched them cheekily before hopping away. They laughed.

They made their way to the subway station. There was a hustling, pushing crowd eager to get home.

"We'll take this one," Barbara said, as a train drew up. "You'll need to push. There'll be room, even if it doesn't look like it."

The carriage doors opened, the crowd surged forward, and

they were swept into a compartment. There were no vacant seats, so Barbara and Keith clung to straps above their heads. As the train drew away, its motion pushed them all together, close; and at each stop the crowd swayed as passengers forced their way on or off. People were good-humoured and laughed, but Keith found it a relief to step out of the train at the other end.

Barbara's apartment was on the third floor. The entrance was off a passageway lined with doors of other apartments. Inside, it was small but comfortably furnished and contained a kitchenette, a round table with a vase of flowers on it, a bed, and a divan that could be converted into another bed. The windows at the back brought in a little light, but the view was blocked by another apartment building.

Keith enjoyed the supper. It was a welcome change from casual snacks in services canteens. Afterwards, they relaxed on the divan chatting. Barbara reached across and turned on the radio, changing the stations until she found some light music. He told her he had served in Egypt, but she didn't seem curious about Egypt, or anything else.

She simply said, "Well, after all the places you've been, I'm pleased we met each other."

She offered him another cup of coffee, but he could tell from her voice that she was tired.

He glanced at his watch. "You've got work tomorrow. I'd better be on my way. I'd like to see you again, though."

"How about Saturday? Two o'clock, in Times Square."

They agreed they would go to the new Alfred Hitchcock film.

Barbara fetched his greatcoat. "You'll need this. It's a cool night."

He buttoned it up and then turned to her. "May I kiss you goodnight?"

She smiled. "You Englishmen are so formal."

"Englishman!" he said in mock horror. "Haven't you been listening to me at all? Anyway, I'll take that as a yes." He reached across, tracing his finger gently on her cheek. Her skin felt soft. She wore very little make-up. He liked that. And she had a dusting of freckles across her nose. He breathed in the light perfume she wore, then leaned closer and kissed her on the lips.

The two of them spent a lot of time together after that. Keith would often fill in the days at her apartment and they would eat a meal together when she got home. At weekends they would go on outings together. She was pleasant company and undemanding.

On Monday and Wednesday evenings Barbara had an evening class at Brooklyn College, and he went there once to meet her. She emerged with a stream of others, men as well as women, many of them dark-haired and dark-eyed, some of the men in skullcaps.

Her face lit up when she saw him and she linked her arm through his. "Come on, I'll show you around."

They walked across to the quadrangle towards the library building with its tall tower.

In a diner Keith came across a copy of the *Brooklyn Daily Eagle* dated September 23, 1943, and, thinking of Walter Simon, he began reading it. The front page headline read Nazis scuttle ships, fire piers at Naples. Even the local content was mostly war-related: a *Superman* cartoon urging people to buy war bonds; a photo of a woman working on her thirty-first pair of woollen socks for boys overseas; a German alien arrested by the FBI on charges of falsely claiming American citizenship in seeking war plant jobs.

Keith searched the newspaper for articles by Walter but found none.

Chapter 12

Barbara sat stiffly beside Keith on the ferry. He had made several attempts at conversation, but she had answered in monosyllables. It was early December and they had been to New Jersey to visit her folks for the day. They had caught the ferry across the Hudson and then a local train. Now the ferry approached Manhattan on their return to the city.

"What's wrong, Barbara?" he finally asked.

"Nothing."

"There is." He glanced at her and saw that her brow was furrowed and her lips set. "You're cross with me, aren't you?"

She said nothing.

"It's something I did at your parents' place, isn't it?"

Still she said nothing.

"They did their best to make me feel at home."

She turned to him and said quietly, "Did their best. That's exactly it. Their best wasn't good enough for you, was it?"

"That's unfair. I remembered my manners, if nothing else."

"I'm not talking about manners, and you know it. You thought they were beneath you, didn't you?"

"Of course I didn't. Why should I? I come from a humble enough background myself."

But he knew there was an element of truth in what she said. Despite himself, he had compared Barbara's parents to Vi and Art, who were comfortably off and accustomed to foreign visitors. He felt ill at ease with her parents and unable to relax. Both sides had struggled to find topics of common interest. This was mostly his fault. So much of his past life remained off limits, he was always on his guard.

Keith continued, "It takes me a while to get to know people. I'm sorry if I appeared distant." Barbara had fallen into silence again, and he tried to meet her eyes. "The last thing I want to do is hurt you."

She spoke then, her voice small and sad. "You have a strange way of showing it, Keith."

He sensed that she was waiting for him to say something else. But he had nothing more to say, nothing of any significance. And so he simply said, "We're both tired. We had an early start this morning. I'll walk you to the subway. On Wednesday I'll come and meet you after your class."

She gave him an unfathomable look and said nothing more.

After taking Barbara to the subway, Keith tramped the streets. He realised that his relationship with her had reached a turning point. The awkward visit to her parents had been a symptom of a larger problem: his need to conceal aspects of his past meant he could not relax with people, could not be honest with them. During the course of his friendship with Barbara he had told her much about his early life, but little about his time in America. She never questioned his unlimited furlough. He had no idea what her conclusions were. There was another complication, too. The girl who shared her apartment was due back in a few days. She might have a more inquisitive nature than Barbara.

It was dark now, and cold, so he turned up his collar and pushed his hands deep into his pockets. He needed warmer clothes; however, his funds were low. He could try to find work, but he could hardly turn up in uniform. There was little chance of getting civilian clothes, and in any event they might pull him up as a draft dodger.

For the first time he allowed himself the thought, *Perhaps I should give myself up*. But what would happen after that? He was a deserter, well beyond AWOL. He would be arrested and sent back to England. What then? Court-martial? The Glasshouse at Aldershot?

A wave of panic rose from the pit of his stomach and swept over him. Aldershot was almost as bad as Mustafa in Egypt. He'd heard what they said about it. *Makes ordinary prison seem like a holiday. Worse than basic training. You get marched round and round the compound. It's the other prisoners you need to watch out for. A mate of mine knew someone who had his eye gouged out.* And the rest of the time, confined to a tiny cell. He would go mental there.

His heart was pounding, his chest felt tight. He forced himself to breathe slowly and deeply, and gradually he calmed down. Looking around him, he realised he had walked further along Fifth Avenue than he intended and was well into the shopping area. The Christmas displays in the shop windows caught his attention. They were skilfully lit, and each one offered something fresh. The smaller shops might have a simple nativity scene or a tiny gift-wrapped box, while the larger windows featured elaborate displays: bewhiskered, red-coated men, sledges pulled by reindeer or straining huskies, cottages with children tucked up in bed, and mountains of parcels in Christmas wrapping paper. There would be nothing like it anywhere else in the world. In London or Paris the lights would be dim or extinguished and the windows bare or shuttered. He suddenly thought of Jeanne and how much she would have loved these displays. It had been at least six months since he had written to her, but he could hardly do so at present. A feeling of melancholy settled on him, and he remembered the day in Halifax when he and Joe had stepped down the gangway, burdened only by their haversacks. How different his life would have been if he had remained in port that day.

A clock struck the hour, and he turned to walk up the avenue towards his billet. He had been lucky here. He had a good comfortable bed, a free one, in what had formerly been a large private home just off Madison Avenue and near Central Park. It had been taken over by a private club in order to provide sleeping accommodation for servicemen.

A small box for voluntary contributions sat on a table at the foot of the stairs. Keith pushed a coin into the slot and climbed up to his room. With images of the festive window displays still in his mind, he pondered Christmas Day. It should be spent with congenial company. Barbara would go to New Jersey and he would be alone unless he could find a service club where there was a celebration. He suddenly thought of Vi and Art, and their home upstate. He had not written to them. He dared not, because he was supposed to be in Canada. But he knew they would welcome him with open arms even if he arrived without warning. Visiting them had its risks. They might have other guests, servicemen, who would ask questions. But it was better than staying in New York. Aye, he would go to Vi and Art for Christmas.

Chapter 13

Albany, New York
December 1943

If Vi and Art were surprised at Keith's sudden arrival two days before Christmas, they did not show it. They hugged him warmly and said they were delighted at the prospect of a full house.

That evening the three of them sat chatting in the fire nook. The grate was laid with logs but was unlit. Vi said they did not need it for warmth. They had central heating after all. But they would light it on Christmas Eve to create atmosphere.

Now, looking across at Keith, Vi said, "That wedge cap of yours and your footwear don't give you much protection against the cold. It's a wonder they let you leave camp dressed like that. Surely they've issued you with winter gear?"

He thought quickly. "They were issuing winter kit when I left camp. There was some red tape and delays. I was keen to get away for Christmas, so I slipped through the inspection."

"I would have thought they'd supply it before December, especially up north," Art said.

Keith did not have a response. He stared at the logs in the grate.

"Keith, I—" Vi checked herself and continued in a lighter tone, "At least your uniform's thick, and you have your greatcoat. But you do need to appreciate the severity of our winters."

The following day another guest arrived: Tom, an English sailor whose ship was in Boston for repairs. Keith breathed more freely after hearing he had been nowhere near the African theatre. When Tom asked what he was doing at present, Keith used the same story he had told Vi and Art. As long as he did not specify a precise locality in Canada he was probably safe.

Tom went out in the late afternoon to meet up with friends, saying he would see everyone in the morning. He had already indicated that he would return to Boston on Boxing Day. Keith felt relieved he would need to spend only one day with him. Tom seemed pleasant enough, but there was always the chance he would ask an awkward question.

In the evening, Art and Vi closeted themselves in the sitting room to decorate the tree. Art emerged two hours later and, with much ceremony, led Keith into the room, which was in complete darkness. He flicked a switch and Keith gasped. The tall balsam in the corner glimmered and shone, its branches hung with lanterns, miniature stockings and coloured lights in green, red and gold. He had never seen anything like it. There had been a Christmas tree one year at the estate owner's house, at a party for the local school children. Jeanne's eyes had lit up with delight. But that was public patronage; this was a family home. He sank into the easy chair by the radio, mesmerised.

Art lit the logs in the grate and the flames began to sparkle. The three of them sat, still and quiet, in a darkness broken only by the fairy lights in the corner and the flickers of the flames. Keith felt suspended in time, and he pushed troubled thoughts of past and future out of his head.

Next morning someone rapped on Keith's door, calling out "Merry Christmas!"

He could hear people moving around, and he checked his watch. It was after nine. He wriggled his feet into a pair of Art's slippers, put on the dressing gown that hung behind the door, then went downstairs.

In the sitting room Tom knelt on the carpet, pulling wrapping paper off a gift. He greeted Keith and pointed to the pile of presents alongside his at the foot of the tree. Each parcel was secured with a narrow ribbon topped with a bow, attached to which was a card with his name on it. He carefully unwrapped each one. There were thick socks, writing paper and envelopes, a handknitted vest, handkerchiefs and a variety of small novelties. Vi and Art brought in coffee and orange juice, and Keith felt a pang. They were kind and warm-hearted, and he was deceiving them.

During the morning, friends of Vi and Art arrived. Then shortly after noon the whole group sat down at the table. Vi had cooked a turkey dinner with mashed potatoes, green beans, gravy and squash, and she had even managed a Christmas pudding as a treat for Tom and Keith. Towards the end of the meal she handed Tom a bottle of rum. He poured a little over the pudding and lit it with a match. The flame curled and licked around the pudding, burning for a while before it flickered out. The party around the table applauded in high spirits.

After the pudding, Vi entertained them with tales about the services canteen where she volunteered. "My friend Claire's a clever mimic. She used to listen to religious programmes, the revivalist type, on the radio each afternoon. Then she'd perform her version for the boys at night, complete with booming voice and dramatic gestures. One sailor who was here for almost two weeks came in whenever she was on duty, asking her to do her act."

"We must ask Claire to make a guest appearance at our church," one of the women joked. "It might stop my husband from falling asleep."

"Oh, Claire has moved on from impersonating preachers," Vi said. "Her current specialty is *Arsenic and Old Lace*. Ever since she saw the play on Broadway, she's been acting the part of a homicidal spinster aunt. She ends her act by charging up the stairs, saluting and then descending with great dignity. The more applause she gets, the more she hams it up."

Keith became aware that the elderly man on his right was speaking to him. "So you come from across the water? I have to admit I haven't always got on with the English."

"I quite understand," Keith said. "I'm a Scot."

"Oh." The man frowned. "The trouble with you Scots is that you let England bully you around, trample all over you. They only tried it once with us." He leaned over to Keith. "My forebears helped chase those damned redcoats out of this country. They ran so fast they never stopped until they reached the St Lawrence. And ever since, the English have never been able to win a war without calling on us for assistance."

Keith shifted in his chair. "Actually, you remind me of a certain kind of Englishman."

The man looked at him warily.

"You'll find him in an exclusive club, and he'll have a little military moustache. He'll sip his whisky and soda and then turn to his neighbour and say, 'You know, old chap, those damned Russians are going a bit too far. Dash it all. It's not cricket, old man. Now when I was in Poona—'"

"I've found people to be much the same wherever you go," Art said, flashing a warning glance at Keith. "Whether they're Scottish nationalists, patriotic Americans, English, Canadian, French … Once you get to know them, you find they all have basically the same hopes and ideals. What do you say, Keith?"

Keith grinned. Art was right: Christmas dinner was no time to get engaged in a petty argument. He raised his glass and said, "Let's drink to the things that unite us."

On New Year's Eve Keith and the Spauldings drove across town to a house party. A man wearing a tartan bow tie played the piano, some of the young ones danced, and there was jollity and laughter. Mrs Stuart, the lady whom Keith had met on his first visit to Albany, was also there and joined their group. The conversation soon turned to Hogmanay in Scotland and the custom of first footing, whereby visitors did their rounds from house to house, seeking to be the first to cross the threshold in the new year.

Keith found it bittersweet to talk to a fellow Scot. It reminded him that he had lost his accustomed surroundings and the whole context in which his life existed. Yet it was a help of sorts to chat to someone with links to that former life.

During a lull in the discussion, Art turned to Keith. "Well, there aren't many days left now before you have to leave." He frowned. "I'm not so keen on you hitchhiking back, not at this time of year anyway."

"Don't worry," Keith said. "It's surprising the amount of traffic that still goes through. I'll try to get something that's going all the way."

"I still don't like it. You don't understand what our winter can be like."

"Well, my luck's usually good. Remember last time I set out to return to Quebec? I'd only been at the intersection for about five minutes when I was picked up by a truck going all the way to Montreal. The same thing—"

"Now I recall what I wanted to say to you," broke in Mrs Stuart. "I passed you at the intersection that morning. I was in a blue car. I slowed down and waved and called out to you, but I don't think you noticed me. I was heading north and intended to offer you a lift. But what surprised me was that you got in a truck going in the opposite direction, towards New York City."

Keith's heart beat fast. He took a moment to collect himself, then he shook his head. "It must have been someone else. From a distance, the uniforms of the different allied troops are similar."

Her eyes flicked up, quick and sharp. "I could have sworn it was you."

"Maybe I've got a double."

She gave him a searching look. Then she said, "Perhaps I was mistaken. It was all over quite quickly." She smiled and turned to Vi. "If the truth be known, he's probably got a young lassie tucked away in New York City and he slips down to see her on the quiet."

Vi smiled in return, but said nothing.

"I wouldn't be surprised if he has," laughed Art. "But Keith's right. It's easy to confuse the uniforms. The Canadian and British ones are almost the same."

When they arrived home, Vi was unusually quiet. She went into the kitchen, returning with a snack for Keith. He sipped the milk and picked up his fork to eat the apple pie.

She started talking in a low voice. "I know there's something wrong, Keith. You lack winter clothing, and you seem to be able to extend your periods of leave at will. If you've got a problem, I'm sure it would do you good to talk it over. Art and I won't judge you. All we want to do is help." She stopped, waiting for him to speak.

Keith shook his head. "There's nothing wrong." He tried to keep his voice light. "You and Art are good friends to me. Can we talk more in the morning?" He rose from his seat and slowly climbed the stairs, taking a hesitant look back at Vi.

That night Keith lay in bed and thought things over. He had reached a turning point. He would either have to tell Vi and Art the truth or break with them completely. He knew he could trust them, but was it fair to ask them to aid a deserter? He smiled wryly to himself. Perhaps he had inherited some of his father's stubbornness and pride.

Next morning, early, before the rest of the household stirred, he was on the road again.

Chapter 14

New York City
January 1944

On his first visits, Keith had become acquainted with one New York City: a city of straight-lined streets and tall, clean buildings; a city that spelled modernity and efficiency; a city that offered hospitality. Now he saw its other face: the drunks in the gutters of the Bowery; the shabby, pleading men who hung around outside second-rate bars; and the ragged children who roamed in gangs. He had observed children like these on city streets and wharves in the Middle East. Art was right. New York City had two faces.

One evening he stood on a street corner listening to the rattle of the elevated railway. Snow carpeted the ground, but it was firm and crisp and the wind had dropped. He had just been to visit Barbara. Their relationship had settled into friendship with no romantic expectations on either side.

"Excuse me, bud. Do you have a light?" Another soldier, a Canadian, had stopped beside him. He was spruce and upright, and Keith saw him give a quick, appraising glance at his uniform. A practised eye would detect how shabby it had become.

Keith felt in his tunic pocket for the packet he'd picked up at a club and struck a match. The soldier offered him a cigarette, introducing himself as Wilson. The two fell into step together.

"I was about to stop for a snack. Let me get you one too," Wilson said.

Keith wished he could reject the offer. Once again he would

need to spin stories and parry questions. But he felt hungry, so he said, "Thanks."

They found a diner that was warm and clean, and he ate his fill of ham and eggs, washed down with plenty of coffee.

Wilson asked, "Been in New York long?"

"I'm just finishing a week's leave. What about you?"

"Arrived today."

Keith quickly took control of the conversation by recommending sights to see and places to go. However, the moment arrived when Wilson asked, "Where are you based?"

"I'm at Borden, in Canada."

"Hmm. I know a guy there."

Damn. Why did I say Borden? I'll need to change the subject. Keith gazed out the window at the snow-covered pavement. "Some of the boys hate the snow and cold up in Canada, but not me. I'm used to it." He moved on to winter sports, and snowstorms in Scotland, and after a while he said, "Sorry, I need to be on my way now. Early train tomorrow."

"Right."

Wilson tossed some coins on the counter and followed him outside. "Which way are you heading?" he asked.

"The other side of Madison Square."

Wilson fell into step beside him and they walked along Madison Avenue and into the square. A gust of wind blew across the square, stirring up the snow at their feet into a fine shower. Keith shivered, and asked himself how he could get back to his room without Wilson following him the whole way.

He came to a halt and then, turning to Wilson, held out his hand and said firmly, "Thanks for the company and for the meal. Enjoy the rest of your stay."

To his relief, Wilson shook his hand without further questions, allowing the two of them to go their separate ways.

Keith came to rely increasingly on the free coffee and donuts at the smaller, scattered canteens. He began to suffer physically because of the life he led, and his skin erupted in blotches and pimples. He became irritable and melancholy by turn, and as time passed he felt the cold more and more. His one change of clothing began to hang on him, which dejected him too, because he was usually meticulous about his appearance. From time to time he glimpsed newspaper headlines about the war—VI Corps, US Fifth Army lands at Anzio … Siege of Leningrad is lifted— and he turned away.

His original funds were gone, so he tried to earn some money. He contacted the proprietors of fun parlours and bowling alleys, tramping from one to the other telling them all the same story: his leave had cost him a lot and he was short in pocket. Often they looked disbelieving and told him to clear out or they would call a cop; but sometimes they gave him a job for a few days setting up pins, monitoring the machines or giving change, or just sweeping and cleaning up.

He considered taking a more permanent job. There would be plenty around, especially with the wartime labour shortage. But even if he got rid of his uniform and replaced it with civilian clothes he would arouse suspicion, especially with his accent. And there might be forms to fill in, regulations to adhere to, check-ups—official attempts to flush out draft dodgers.

When all else failed he resorted to hocking his gear, and he held tickets that he had little hope of redeeming. His wristwatch, his fountain pen and his signet ring went. It was hard to part with them, but money had to come from somewhere.

One morning he lingered in front of the pawnshop that he had visited all too frequently. It occupied the ground floor of one half of a three-storey building with wooden dormers and a chimney on top. Keith wondered if the pawnbroker lived up there. He seemed to be open at all hours. The middle floor of the building had the distinctive pawnbroker's cluster of three balls hanging above it, while every inch of available space was painted in bold lettering: Loan Office, Diamonds, Watches. Between the two tall windows was the name "H. Berkowitz" and another three balls. The shop window, which was crowned with even more clusters of balls, was packed full of goods.

He took from his pocket the brooch that Jeanne had given him, and turned it over in his hand, imagining the interaction that would transpire inside the shop.

It's a pretty thing, but not valuable. I can give you ten dollars against it.

He would try to argue. *Come on, it's worth more than that.*

After a further brief exchange, the pawnbroker would say firmly, *Ten dollars. It's my final offer.*

Keith braced himself and stepped inside. The interior of the shop had a table and shelves, all of which were piled high with toasters, cameras and the residue of people's lives. There were also a few display cases showing jewellery and other small items. The pawnbroker, who had dark, thinning hair and a noticeable paunch, was counting cash. He indicated with his hand that Keith should wait until he had finished. After double-checking his figures, he stowed away the money before addressing Keith.

"How are you?"

"I'm okay, but I'm a bit short of funds."

"Aren't we all? What have you brought me today then?"

Keith studied the brooch. This was his last link to Jeanne; this and a crumpled letter. Sometimes he could barely picture her face.

The pawnbroker addressed him again. "Well?"

Keith hesitated. Then he suddenly registered what he had been about to do. He pushed the brooch back into his pocket. "I've changed my mind," he said.

The pawnbroker shrugged his shoulders as Keith walked out the door.

Keith was always conscious of the risk of being detected. Sometimes he lay on his bed with his eyes wide open and imagined the creak of boots on the stairs, advancing closer and closer. They had found him. Any moment now, the heavy shoulder would thrust against his door. When out and about he always watched for military police, but one afternoon he dropped his guard.

He was on his way to a bowling alley where he had been promised casual work and was deep in his own thoughts amongst a jostling throng of pedestrians. He looked up, straight into the cold eyes of a military police officer who was approaching from the opposite direction accompanied by another officer. The man was powerfully built and swaggered along in white-gaitered boots, a smart khaki uniform with a white webbing belt, and a white-lettered, black armband that shouted MP. Keith saw the officer look him up and down.

He's suspicious. He's noticed my uniform is almost falling apart.

He forced himself to keep walking, eyes straight ahead, but his heart raced as he waited for a sharp command and a hand on his shoulder.

He was still jumpy when he made his way down the stairs to the bowling alley. It was a long windowless area one floor below street level, with concrete walls and big lights hanging from the ceiling to illuminate the four lanes. The proprietor, Mike, was a sharply dressed man in a white shirt and a waistcoat.

His eyes flicked up and down Keith's uniform and he asked, "Haven't you got anything else to wear?" He disappeared, returning almost immediately holding a sweater, which he threw at Keith. "Put that on," he said.

Keith began setting up pins. He knew Mike was watching him, and he sensed that Mike guessed exactly what he was and had employed him only because he was short-staffed.

Four hours later, he was tidying up at the end of his shift when he spotted two military police descending the stairs at the other end of the bowling lanes. The two men were a menacing presence, with long batons and pistols at their sides. As they swept the room with their eyes, Keith realised they were the pair he had seen on the street earlier that day. If they had been suspicious of him then, they would be in no doubt now. He felt himself break into a sweat.

Mike glanced in his direction, then greeted the two officers and began talking to them. Keith lowered his head and continued working, but he had a sick feeling in the pit of his stomach. After what seemed an age, the two officers departed.

Mike strolled over to him and said in a low voice, "I persuaded them I had no one here who would interest them. But I can't afford to invite trouble. I'll pay you what you've earned, and then I want you to scram."

Keith did not attempt to argue. He knew he was beginning to attract attention. The noose was tightening round his neck; it would be only a matter of time.

Chapter 15

Keith could not believe what he saw ahead of him on the footpath. The figure was unmistakeable: tall and well built, tight curly ginger hair, cap rolled up on the shoulder, khaki Australian Army uniform. Keith's heart lifted and he quickened his step until he was just behind the man.

"Joe," he called.

There was no response.

He drew level with him. "Joe."

The big Australian turned his head and Keith met the eyes of a man unknown to him.

"I'm sorry. I thought you were someone else," Keith said.

"No worries, mate. Hope you find him."

A wave of loneliness and loss swept over Keith. He contemplated what might have been. If he had not agreed to accompany Blue and Stretch on their little jaunt. If he had not made that fateful decision at the wharf. If he had not run away.

One Sunday evening in late February Keith was walking up Madison Avenue towards his billet. The sound of bagpipes drifted from a building that had lights on upstairs, and he saw the outline of people's heads through the windows. Perhaps they were celebrating something.

Hunching his shoulders, he put his head down against the cold. The street was quite dark and there were few people around.

As he passed a large doorway, a man emerged from the shadows and spoke, the smell of stale cigarette smoke on his breath.

"Got a light on you?"

Keith paused and felt in his pocket. Suddenly the man shoved him against the building. In his hand, up near Keith's throat, gleamed a stout-bladed knife.

"Give me your wallet."

Keith tensed like a cat. For the first time in months his mind was crystal clear. His feelings of inertia, indecision and panic were gone. In an instant he summed up his opponent. Slim build, same height as himself, just as pale and unhealthy looking. And currently holding the advantage. In the absence of a weapon or anything he could improvise as a one, he had two options: hand over the wallet, or surprise the man into dropping the knife and then take to his heels.

Keith slowed his breathing and spoke in a calm, relaxed voice. "Let me get it for you. I don't want any trouble." He started to move his right hand, slowly, as if to his pocket. His opponent relaxed his stance slightly.

Now! He grabbed the man's wrist with his left hand and rotated it sharply in a clockwise direction, pressing downward so the bones cracked. "Drop that knife or I'll break your wrist," he hissed.

"Aah!" the man exclaimed in pain and surprise and reeled back, clutching his wrist, as the knife clattered to the ground.

With a fluid movement Keith slid away. Then he walked briskly to his billet without looking behind him.

Before he went to bed he packed his meagre gear into his kitbag. He had made a decision. It was time to swallow his pride and face reality. Tomorrow early, he would be on the road hitchhiking to Albany. He would tell Vi and Art everything, and between the three of them they might find a solution. At the very least, it would be a relief to share his secret.

That night, for once, he fell asleep quickly.

Keith could hear the wail of bagpipes playing a march. The pipers strode out front, leading a sea of kilted men, and he was among them, calm and proud. They were entering into Egypt, marching into battle. He was with his battalion, where he belonged, and he was joyful.

The bagpipes gradually faded, and he began to hear cars, trucks, voices, bustle, the sounds of New York. He realised that it was dawn, that he had been dreaming, but he retained that sense of quiet joy.

As he opened his eyes and became fully awake, the depressing reality of his life crept back over him. He sighed heavily, pushed the covers off himself and sat up. He swung his legs from the bed and set his feet on the floor. Then he saw his kitbag, packed ready from the night before, and he remembered what he had to do today.

It was now well into winter, and there was little traffic on the roads upstate. The country was cold and stormy, the snow deep and hard, and a bitter wind blew in from the north. Keith struggled along the road, trying to hunch his shoulders and hide his face from the wind. There was no sign of shelter. In his weakened physical state he knew he could not go much further.

As a hitchhiker in winter weather, he had made a rookie mistake. Instead of waiting in town for a lift that would take him all the way, he had jumped at the first offer. The motorist had gone perhaps ten miles out of town and then pulled up shortly before an intersection, turning to Keith with a puzzled look.

"You said you wanted to keep to the main highway?"

"That's right."

"In this weather?"

"Aye."

The motorist shrugged his shoulders. "This is as far as I can take you. I turn off here. Good luck. You'll need it."

The crosswind cut through and chilled. Keith twisted his back towards it as best he could, turned up his collar and jammed his hands deep into his pockets. His greatcoat and cap provided little protection in these conditions. Small flurries of snow swirled around him. The wind shrieked, and his face grew numb. His steps slowed.

He scarcely heard the truck draw up beside him, and he needed the firm grasp of the driver to help him clamber aboard. The man glanced at him occasionally as he drove on, but he said little, and Keith half dozed. In the warmth of the cab he began to feel sharply those patches of flesh that had been exposed to the cold.

After a while, the truck driver pulled off the main highway and turned into the yard of a canning factory. "This is where I work, son. Hop down, and we'll take you inside to warm you up."

He took Keith down to the basement of the factory. Men in overalls and two young women were eating lunch, and they looked at Keith curiously. One of them brought him a hot drink, which he sipped cautiously.

The group resumed eating their lunch, but he felt he owed them an explanation and so he said, "I'm based in Borden and have been on leave in New York City. I spent all my money. Otherwise I'd be travelling by railroad. I appreciate the help you've given me. If someone could give me a lift to the nearest town, I'll start hitching north from there."

The truck driver said, "Take your time, son. You need to warm up properly before we'll let you go anywhere."

The truck driver wandered over to one of the young women and led her out of the room. Ten minutes later the two of them returned, the woman with an envelope in her hand.

"Do you feel warmer now?" the truck driver asked.

"Much better."

"I've got a son about your age," the man said. "He's serving overseas. I like to think that if he got in a bind, and I wasn't there to help him, someone else would. Julie here has taken up a collection among the office staff and some of the men."

As Keith started to protest, the driver continued firmly, "No arguments. If you go out on that road, you'll never see home again. There's enough money in this envelope to get you a good solid meal and a train ticket back to your base. One of our drivers will take you to the station. He's waiting out there now."

Chapter 16

Albany, New York
February 1944

Keith arrived in Albany with cash to spare and found Vi and Art both at home when he rang the front doorbell. They said little about his unexpected return, but he could see they were shocked at his appearance. He was aware that his face was thin and grey, his battledress soiled and damp.

Vi warmed up some chicken fricassee for him, and she and Art sat down at the table too, each with a cup of coffee.

Keith looked first at Vi and then at Art. "I think you've already guessed that I haven't been telling you the whole truth."

"All in good time, son," Art said. "Get some of that hot food inside you first."

Keith ate the chicken, then positioned his knife and fork carefully on his plate, adjusting them until they were parallel.

Art glanced at Vi before addressing Keith. "Tell us what happened, son."

Keith chose his words carefully at first, through long habit. "The story about North Africa is true. I was the only survivor when our bren carrier ran over a landmine." He gave Vi and Art a brief account of how he had voyaged to Halifax, encountered Blue and Stretch in a services canteen, then left the port with them. "I got back to Halifax after two days."

His heart started racing, pounding in his chest. "I got back to Halifax, and the ship was still at the pier preparing to leave." The words stuck in his throat, but he forced himself to continue. "I was standing beside the wharf building. I intended to board the ship, but suddenly there was a terrible scream. It sounded like my friend Jimmy dying there in North Africa, calling out to me …" His voice faded away.

Vi and Art waited, until at last Art said, "Go on, son."

"At that instant, something changed inside my head. I can't explain why, but—" His voice caught, and he took his time to regain control. "I stood there and watched the ship sail away."

"What happened next?" Art asked.

"I …" Keith bent his head. "I …" He put his face in his hands and began weeping, his shoulders shaking.

After a moment or two, Vi reached over and laid her hand on Keith's arm. "It's good for you to cry. You've been bottling this up for so long."

Gradually Keith became calmer. He looked up, rubbing his eyes. Art passed him his handkerchief.

He gave them a full account of what had happened since that day in Halifax. The coffee in the cups grew cold while Art's cigarette went out and he did not light another.

When Keith had finished speaking, there was silence for a while and then Art stirred.

"We wondered if something was wrong, even on your first visit to us. If we'd asked more questions, learned the truth, we'd have encouraged you to turn yourself in, before your status changed from AWOL to deserter."

"Hindsight's a fine thing," Vi said. She touched Keith's arm. "You're exhausted. Let's all get some rest. We'll talk more tomorrow."

That night, Keith had a deep and dreamless sleep, the first in a long time. It was after midday when he woke up. Vi had left a note on the kitchen table:

Keith,

Hope you had a good long sleep. Fix yourself a snack. Bacon and eggs in the refrigerator, or more chicken fricassee if you can stand it. I'll be home from work early (am on 9 to 3 schedule this week).

Vi

He was still at the table when Vi arrived home. "Sleep well?" she asked.

"Aye, I've only recently got up." He leaned back in his chair, stretching his arms up in the air. "I've been enjoying the warmth and looking out on to the yard. The sun on the snow was almost blinding a wee bit earlier. It's hard to believe I was caught in a blizzard twenty-four hours ago."

"This unexpected sunshine has given me the spring urge," Vi said. "Next thing you know, I'll be studying seed catalogues and planning the flower garden."

She made a pot of coffee, and sat at the table opposite Keith. "You look a lot better than you did yesterday."

"Amazing what a decent night's sleep can do. And it's a load off my mind being able to talk to someone. I couldn't go on any longer the way I was. It wasn't living; it was barely existing."

"I realise you want to make decisions about your future," Vi said, "but Art and I both think you should concentrate on regaining your health first. What have you been eating lately? Your skin's in a bad state."

"Black coffee and doughnuts. After I ran out of money, that's all I ate for weeks. Free at the services canteens."

"Oh dear. Well, a few weeks of home cooking will fix that." She studied his face. "One thing that *has* improved is your eyes. The pupils are back to normal. Before, they were dilated all the time."

"I seem to have recovered from my concussion at last."

Vi frowned. "You might have recovered from the knock on the head, but over there in the desert you suffered a mental trauma too. You lost your best friends, all at once. That kind of thing affects you, whether you admit it or not. I'm a hospital pharmacist, not a psychiatrist, but I've hosted numerous young soldiers, and I recognise the signs. It's called battle fatigue."

Keith shrugged. "Do you mean the nightmares? I don't have them much any more."

"These things have a habit of returning unbidden unless you look them in the face."

In the following days Vi kept probing, forcing Keith to open up, to talk to her about people, places, events that had been significant to him. He found himself telling her about his early life, the death of his mother, the estrangement from his father, and also his brother's fatal fall.

"You blame yourself too much," Vi said. "It seems to me that your brother's death wasn't anyone's fault. It was a boyish adventure that went tragically wrong."

She asked him to talk about the night of the Bren Carrier explosion, and he told her what little he recollected. Then he described the terrifying flashback he had at the port in Halifax.

"You know deep down, don't you, that there's nothing you could have done to save your friends?"

"Aye."

"Terrible things happen in war, often without rhyme or reason. It's not your fault that you survived and the others didn't."

It was late afternoon, and Keith and Art had settled themselves into two old armchairs in Art's den, a narrow room at the back of the house. Beside Art's chair stood a small table with a bottle of whiskey and glasses. He poured two shots and handed one to Keith.

"Try this, and tell me what you think. It's a Kentucky straight rye."

Keith sniffed the whiskey. "Spicy." He took a long, slow sip. "Cinnamon and cloves. And it's quite fruity."

"Different from your single malts?"

"Aye." He took another sip of the whiskey, and the warmth crept down to his stomach and suffused his body.

Art rolled his glass in his hands. "You said you wanted to talk through your options with me."

Keith nodded. "I've had enough of being isolated, depressed, always looking over my shoulder. Now that I'm away from New York I feel better already, but I can't stay with you and Vi forever."

"Agreed. Much as we enjoy having you." Art took his time before he continued. "As I see it, you've got three possibilities."

"I'd thought of two. Go on."

"There's the obvious choice. Return to Halifax and give yourself up."

Keith frowned. "I could do that, but it would mean a court-martial and a lengthy term in the Glasshouse. I can't say I don't deserve it though." He paused. "There's another thing. This might sound odd coming from a man who's been running from the authorities for the past year, but I don't relish being safely locked up while my mates might be dying."

Art nodded. "Did you know I was a veteran, of the war that was going to end all wars?"

Keith's eyes widened. "No."

"Only just. I went to France with the American Expeditionary Force in September 1918, and the war ended two months later. I was in the Battle of Argonne Forest. I was shit-scared. We all were." He looked Keith in the eye. "Were you shit-scared out there in the desert?"

"Not really. I built up to it, I suppose. Months of training in Scotland and England, and then in Egypt we had good leaders, good men. I got sick of the heat and the dust, but the army was my whole life."

"You'll never be able to return to your unit, son. But I've got another option for you, something I want you to consider." Art handed him an open magazine. "Read those two pages and tell me what you think."

Keith was silent as he scanned the article, which was about the Willow Run manufacturing complex in Michigan and the mass production of B-24 Liberator heavy bombers.

"The war industry's huge, and they need workers." Art leaned forward. "Do you know in California they've had sound trucks going street by street begging people to apply for jobs?"

"Okay. There's a labour shortage in the war industry. What's that got to do with me?"

"I think you understand what I'm suggesting, Keith."

"Actually, I don't. There's no way I could apply for one of these jobs. They'd ask why I hadn't been drafted, if they even believed I was in the country legally."

Art held up his hand. "Let's speak about this rationally."

"Rationally? I'm sorry, I know you're trying to help, but it's a crazy idea."

"You look very young for your age, Keith. You could probably pass for seventeen."

"What! I don't think so."

"Once you've got your condition back."

"It's too risky. I'd attract attention immediately."

Art shifted in his chair, impatiently. "You're not even giving this a chance. I appreciate it's not the same as being with your old unit, but you'd be doing your bit for the war effort."

Keith sighed heavily. "If they found me out, it would appear as if I'd deserted just to get the money that's going in defence jobs over here."

"You'll need to give me a stronger argument than that, Keith. Since when have you been afraid of taking a risk?"

Keith drained his glass before answering. "Put simply, I don't have the stomach to earn big money at the expense of men who are serving."

Art leaned forward, clasping his hands on his knee. "If you had your choice, given you can't undo the past, and you can't rejoin your unit, what would you like to do? Where would you like to be?"

"I'd like to be back in uniform."

Art did not appear surprised. He waited for a moment. "There's a third option. I promised Vi I'd present it to you last because it makes her a bit fearful. But if you decide it's what you want to do, we'll both support you all the way. He gave a slow smile. "You know how Vi likes helping people. Our own boy died when he was three months old. We couldn't have any more children."

Keith nodded. Vi had mentioned the baby to him once.

"It also involves passing yourself off as younger," Art said, "but this time you'll be eighteen. What I'm saying is that there might be a way you can get into the armed services over here."

"How on earth could I do that?"

"I remember reading a short time ago that up until 1926, or even later, Florida and some of the other southern states didn't keep a complete record of their births."

"Are you suggesting I try to pass myself off as an American and front up for the draft? That's a bit unrealistic, isn't it? I'd be uncovered immediately."

"Well, your only other option, since you don't want to apply for a war job, is to give yourself up. The way I see it, if you're going to face a court-martial in any event, you might as well make a scrap of it first. Vi and I will help you with a backstory and coach you in American ways."

"That'd be a challenge."

Art ignored Keith's remark. "You'd need to lie low. We don't want folks asking questions." He poured another two whiskeys. "You know, you wouldn't be the first man to have passed himself off as an American and fronted up for the draft."

Keith was thoughtful. "Now you mention it, I remember hearing about someone who did that. They were discussing it in one of the services canteens. His true identity was only discovered after he drowned at sea." He sipped his whiskey and sat in silence. At last he spoke again. "Aye. That's what I'll do. Create a new identity and register for the draft. I'd rather die in war than die inside me."

Chapter 17

Brooklyn, New York
April 1944

Keith walked along the street, barely aware of his surroundings. From time to time he glanced at the numbers on the buildings. A young woman with a pram brushed past him and turned to apologise. Her voice was accented—Italian, he thought—and she had dark curly hair. He smoothed back his own hair, which he had let grow longer over the past few weeks so it fell over his forehead.

Not far to go now. He rehearsed everything in his head yet again. *My name is Keith Anderson. I was born in Florida on April 4, 1926. My parents are both dead.* No one was likely to comment on his Scottish brogue, you heard so many different accents around here; but he had an answer prepared if they did ask. *My father was American, but my mother came from Scotland. We went there to live for five years when I was a young child.*

With a jolt he realised he had reached the building he was searching for. His chest suddenly felt constricted and he had trouble breathing. He could not go through with this. He did not have the audacity. *Audacity? Cheek? If only Blue was here with me.* He stood staring at the building.

"Get a move on. You can't hold up business like that," said a voice at his shoulder.

He spun around. The voice sounded familiar but there was no one there.

"Pull your bloody finger out, mate. Get on up there, and stop looking as if a judge is about to pronounce sentence on you. There's nothing to worry about."

"Blue!" Keith exclaimed. However, Blue was nowhere in sight. His mind must be playing tricks on him. But no, there it was again.

"Listen, mate. I can't stick around here all day! Don't you remember what I told you? A little bit of cheek goes a long way. Get it over and bloody done with."

Keith knew that Blue was right. He took a moment to compose himself, to restore his normal rhythm of breathing, then he walked up the steps of the brownstone building. The front door was open, and he could see a flight of stairs and a sign on the wall: SELECTIVE SERVICES BOARD – SECOND FLOOR. He started to climb the stairs.

It had been six weeks since the day he went to Vi and Art and told them the full story. Vi's hearty meals and the rest and recuperation had soon restored his physical health. He felt mentally stronger, too, after long conversations with Vi and Art in which they expressed support and understanding while at the same time forcing him to face his demons. Once Art had ascertained he was correct about the lack of birth certificates in some southern states, Keith had worked out his plan of action. He hocked his uniform in order to put together a civilian outfit, and then Art and Vi gave him intensive coaching.

"If you're going to pose as a Yank, you must talk and act like one," Art had said. "We can't hope to change your accent, but you need to start using American words and expressions."

They drilled him for hours. *Pavement*, *petrol* and *tramcar* became *sidewalk*, *gasoline* and *streetcar*. He fastened his *suspenders*, not his braces. His weight was one hundred and fifty pounds and no longer ten stone ten. The clock said ten after eight, not ten past. At mealtimes he juggled with his fork in his right hand and learned to use his knife as little as possible. Art, seated across the table from him, interrupted him whenever he lapsed into his old ways.

Keith stepped into a small waiting room with straight-backed chairs. Through another closed door he could hear the murmur of voices. He sat down to wait.

A short time later, the door opened and a youth emerged. He nodded at Keith before heading down the stairs.

A man popped his head out saying, "We'll be ready for you shortly," and closed the door again.

Three men were seated behind the table. The one in the centre did most of the talking.

"Name?"

"Keith Anderson."

"Date of birth?"

"April 4, 1926."

"Place of birth."

"Fort Myers, Florida."

The man asked him to speak up.

Keith cleared his throat and managed to get firmer control of his voice. His hands bothered him. At first he held them straight at his sides and stood to attention. Then he bent his right leg slightly and tucked one hand in his pocket so he would look less fidgety. When the man looked up at him, he resumed his straight, upright position and hurriedly withdrew the hand from his pocket. Finally he relaxed both his knees and placed the fingers of each hand lightly on the desk in front of him.

The long-faced man asked Keith a lot of questions, and Keith gave his carefully rehearsed answers. He had no birth certificate. His parents were both dead. Yes, he could provide the name of a person to notify in case of emergency.

"Address?"

He registered his address as the rooming house in Brooklyn where he was staying.

"Occupation?"

This was harder, but his youth helped. "I've been doing casual work. Recently I've worked in fun parlours in the city. Before that I did seasonal work on farms."

He had spent hours preparing for this interview, approached

it from every angle, only to find that the board members did not probe, did not comment on his accent and did not make a fuss about his lack of birth certificate. The board members appeared tired. Keith told himself they had probably spoken to numerous other young men that day, and his file would soon become swamped in thousands of others. He answered more questions, and then suddenly the long-faced man said the interview was at an end.

As Keith walked out of the room he felt exhausted, but he knew he had cleared the stiffest hurdle. The physical examination still to come did not worry him so much. It had been over a year since he had suffered his concussion, and he bore no obvious scars from his other physical injuries.

A few weeks later, "Keith Anderson" sat in a diner, a cup of coffee in front of him.

He and Vi and Art had come up with this name between them. At first they had been at a loss as to what to choose, so they had worked through the names of the American presidents. They had settled on Keith Adams, but then decided Anderson was better. It was a common name like Adams, but it was also one that echoed the rhythm of his real surname. They decided there was no need to change his Christian name because Keith was not his first name according to official records. He had been christened Kenneth Keith Mathieson. Now he was Keith Anderson, and he said this name to himself in the mirror every day when shaving. He practised his new signature time and again.

As he drank his coffee, he looked at the short note he had just written to Vi and Art.

> *Do you remember all my jibes about the Coca-Cola Navy? Well, what do you know. I report next week to boot camp at Bainbridge, Maryland. Even though it's not the service I had wished for, I'm pleased to have succeeded thus far, and I thank you for all your help.*
>
> *Keith Anderson*

His coffee cup was filled up again, and he began leafing through the newspapers that lay on the counter. A *New York Times* headline read TWO THOUSAND US PLANES ATTACK BERLIN AND TWO AIRCRAFT PLANTS NEAR THE CITY. Another paper had a short item about a Welsh soldier who, for reasons that were unclear, had swapped identities with a GI in the United Kingdom. Posing as an American, he had sailed to the United States with the US Army, from which he had promptly deserted. He had subsequently been picked up by the police on an unrelated matter. This story did not spoil Keith's mood. He was realistic about the risks he was taking and the need for caution.

Chapter 18

Bainbridge, Maryland
May 1944

Life in the new service was both easy and difficult for Keith. Unlike his fellow recruits, who had known only civilian life, he took naturally to the drill and the discipline; however, he needed to avoid appearing too efficient; he needed to appear, like the others, to learn as he went along. An additional challenge was that many of the commands and movements differed from those taught in the British Army. He found himself slipping into old ways at times. His saluting, in particular, he found hard to change and he was pulled up on numerous occasions.

Once, an exasperated chief petty officer shouted out to him, "Where the hell did you pick up that salute, Anderson? Anyone would think you were a Limey! Do it the proper way, man!"

His buddies laughed it off. He was not the only one to be chewed out because his salute was not up to scratch.

At first the others ribbed him about his accent, so he gave them his carefully prepared explanation about living in Scotland as a child. He failed at times to understand the expressions they used, and so he kept to himself for the first few days. All the while he watched the other men, learning from them. In the end, what got him accepted by the others was his prowess on the range: he proved himself the crack shot of the outfit.

Ironically, his success on the range led to a worrying interaction with the chief petty officer in charge of their training, a man with some years' experience in handling recruits.

Keith noticed the chief observing him closely and one day, after a successful shoot at the range, he called Keith aside.

"Anderson, I usually have the measure of new recruits by the end of the first week, but you're still a mystery to me. You handle weapons like a veteran. Where did you learn to shoot like that?"

Keith thought quickly. "I used sporting rifles when I was younger, Chief. Also, before I joined up I worked in fun parlours. I usually looked after the shooting gallery and I had plenty of time to practise."

The chief petty officer appeared unconvinced. "No, it's more than that. You outshine the rest of this bunch when you want to, not only on the range but everywhere else. Most times you display none of the awkwardness or the eagerness of the average new recruit. You arrange your kit for inspection neater than anyone else, yet you do it in half the time. It's almost as if you've done it all before." He looked sharply at Keith.

Keith made no comment, and the chief continued, "Most times you give the impression you were born into this discipline and training. Then you suddenly spoil it by executing the wrong movement on the parade ground and throwing the squad into confusion, or performing your rifle drill some fancy way when there's an officer passing, or doing some other God damn stupid thing. Why are you like this, Anderson?"

Keith took a moment to reply. "I've knocked around a lot, Chief, and I've had to fend for myself, for the most part, since my parents died, so I guess that's made me self-reliant. So far as parading is concerned, well, when I was a kid we lived near an old chap who'd been a regular in the British Army, and he used to spin us tales about his ancient battles. We were as keen as anything, and he got us marching round with sticks doing rifle drill. It's funny how the things you learn as a kid stay with you. Sometimes on parade I slip back into the ways this old fella taught us."

He looked at the chief petty officer, thinking how lame his explanation was, but the other, surprisingly, did not question it. Instead he dismissed Keith, saying, "I still don't get it, but as long as you turn out to be a credit to our training, that's all I'm worried about.

The chief never mentioned the subject again.

Keith adjusted rapidly to the remainder of the course and, as he began to fit more easily into the ways of conversation of the younger men, he lost his earlier reticence. His amiable disposition and his skill at gunnery made him generally liked and accepted. He also had the knack of being able to solve many of the minor problems besetting new recruits. He was regarded, despite his youth, almost as the father of the outfit. The shadow in the background, the fear that one day an official check-up would betray him, never quite went away, but he coped with it by telling himself his file was probably hidden among countless others in a maze of officialdom.

At the end of boot camp the men received a few days' leave and they headed straight for New York City. As Keith strolled up Fifth Avenue with the rest of the group, he revelled in the contrast with his previous visits. He wore a different uniform, dress blues and a round white cap. He had money in his pocket, and he could walk the streets confidently, without fear of being apprehended by military police.

They were in a crowd together. The others were trainees from different parts of the country, younger than him, many of them visiting New York City for the first time, all of them with the cockiness of new recruits proud to be in uniform. They stopped in a bar, drinking to the future and to success; and then, in that happy state of mind that follows the consumption of a balanced amount of liquor, they wandered along the street.

As they rounded a corner, they ran into a party of British tars approaching from the opposite direction. There was some back-slapping and hand-pumping, then one of the Yanks who was more inebriated than the others addressed the tars.

"Brothers, your troubles are ended! Once we're over there, the war's as good as won."

"So you're going to win this war too, eh?" said one of the British seamen. He turned to his mates. "Look at them, boys. The Coca-Cola Navy. They're going to win the war for us after lying with their heads under the blankets for the past few years."

The Limeys laughed and one of them called out, "What! No ribbons or decorations yet? Maybe you didn't reach the basketball finals."

Keith, who had been listening with mounting concern as the words flew faster, stepped into the centre to calm the situation. However, it had the opposite effect. He was pushed off balance and in a flash fists were flying all around him. He threw a few punches himself, but his heart was not in it. Once upon a time he would have relished a scrap like this; now he did not even know which side he supported. He wore a Yankee uniform. He had just spent four weeks training with these boys. But the others were his countrymen.

The fight grew wilder, moving from the sidewalk to the street as more men joined in. Keith reeled with the impact of a blow that winded him and made him double up.

Then suddenly a whistle sounded in the distance and someone shouted, "Shore patrol!"

He felt firm hands grasp him, propel him along the street. A voice yelled, "Hurry up! Here they come," and he was hauled into a doorway.

"Quick, in here. We'll wait till they go past," someone said.

"That was a close shave!" another replied.

As his head cleared, he realised to his amusement that he had a Yank to one side of him and a British tar to the other. Ten minutes later they were all in a tavern, Yanks and Limeys, sitting down to hamburgers and coffee, their fight forgotten.

After his leave, Keith was posted to gunnery training school in Norfolk, Virginia, and he wrote to Vi and Art:

Dearest Vi and Art,

Norfolk, VA, is a place God created and promptly forgot, nestled at the mouth of the James River. It seems that, at one time or another, every ship in the proud fleet has come here, much to the disgust of their crews I daresay. The first morning, we were hustled down to an ex-gun boat of 1905 vintage that has been converted into a gunnery training ship for those who will go to sea and man the guns of the merchant ships. But all sarcasm aside (on the subject of Norfolk), we had bags of fun on board the old tub for the next few days. We dashed up and down Chesapeake Bay firing every gun on the ship and frightening the little fishes who inhabit these waters. We all prayed violently that some foolish U-boat would show its head, but we were disappointed (happy to say). We have just arrived back in port and I feel fine, though some of the sailors have noticed the motion of the seas with violent results.

The treats they have in store for us include swimming under burning oil, and also jumping from a diving board with a life jacket on. I believe the secret is to hold the jacket down so it doesn't snap your neck when you hit the water, but I'm sure they'll clarify this for us.

Say hello to my four-leggedy friends for me, and please write. I'm lonely at times and anxious to hear from you. I promise to do everything I can to get ahead while on this course. I may even win the right to have two hooks attached to my sleeve.

Wish you all the very best, and I will write again soon.

I remain yours, with much love.

K.

Chapter 19

New York
June 1944

Keith stood to attention beside his gun on the freighter SS *Harold Beacon* as she steamed slowly down the Hudson River in single file with other merchant ships, all of them on their way to take their assigned positions in a convoy that was forming up for the Persian Gulf. He had completed his training, gained his gunner's mate second stripe and been assigned to the merchant fleet as a naval gunner. His worry about being caught by an official check-up had receded. Today, on his first day out, he felt happy and secure.

It did not bother him that he sailed under the Stars and Stripes rather than the Union Jack. What mattered was being part of a unit again. Now it was the Naval Armed Guard, a team of twenty-five gunners and two signalmen who served under a gunnery officer, Lieutenant (Junior Grade) John Savela, alongside the merchant crew. During combat, Savela would share authority with the ship's captain, but at other times he and the Armed Guard took no part in the operation of the vessel. Their job was to man and maintain their guns.

The *Harold Beacon* was a Liberty ship, mass-produced from prefabricated parts. She had two "big guns," a three-inch 50-calibre gun forward in the point of the bow and a five-inch 38-calibre on the stern, and also eight 20 mm Oerlikon machine guns, one on each corner of the bridge and four on the upper deck. Keith's action station was at one of the starboard Oerlikons on the bridge.

Keith soon became accustomed to the routine of workdays at

sea. He stood watch, four hours on and eight hours off, in a steady rotation with other members of the Naval Armed Guard. In addition to this, each day at 0600 and again at dusk, the most likely times for enemy attack, all hands manned battle stations and the guns were elevated and trained through their full arcs. General training, including loading drills, was held daily, and there were fire and boat drills once a week. Lieutenant Savela made daily inspections of the ammunition storage magazines and the ready boxes next to the guns, and all guns were regularly cleaned and lubricated. The Armed Guard performed tasks such as painting in their down time.

Living conditions on the *Harold Beacon* were good. In the mess, the men could select from the menu on the board and the meal would be brought out and set out in front of them. One of the gunners said, only half joking, that this was why he had volunteered for the Armed Guard. And unlike navy men on warships, they were permitted to wear informal clothing, dungarees, during their workday.

When he was not working or sleeping, Keith read, wrote letters, played cards with the navy and merchant crew, and undertook a physical fitness regime, jogging and lifting weights in confined spaces. He washed out his clothes in a bucket and hung them to dry in the engine room, becoming friendly with the "black gang" who worked down there, in particular the oilers, Woodie, Ollie and Chuck. The *Harold Beacon* had a reciprocating steam engine, steady and reliable, and the oilers did their rounds every half-hour, lubricating the bearings of the main engine and its auxiliaries.

Lieutenant Savela was a tall, soft-spoken, sandy-haired man with a calm, quietly authoritative manner. He was well liked by his men, most of whom were young, eighteen or nineteen years old, and fresh from boot camp followed by gunnery instruction at Little Creek.

Early on, Savela told them, "I'm not only your commanding officer. I'm your chaplain and your doctor too." He also reminded them, "The guns on the *Harold Beacon* are defensive. She will always be the hunted, never the hunter."

The Naval Armed Guard were berthed on the boat deck in order to be close to their assigned guns, and Keith shared cramped quarters in the midship area with six others. These men all came from the north-east of the United States with the exception of Denis Thurman, who was from Jacksonville, Florida. Thurman was older than the others, nearer Keith's own age, his real age, and had been in the navy for two years. He wore no stripes on his sleeve despite being competent on the guns, and Keith could only assume he had blotted his copybook in some way. Thurman's action station, like Keith's, was one of the Oerlikons on the bridge.

As one of three ranking enlisted men under Lieutenant Savela's command, Keith was given the role of overseeing all eight Oerlikons. He took his responsibilities seriously, insisting that these rapid-firing anti-aircraft guns be cleaned every day and kept in top condition. Thurman always paused for a fraction before following any of Keith's instructions; not enough to be uncooperative but enough to indicate *I don't have to do this*. Sometimes Keith noticed Thurman watching him as if waiting for him to make a mistake. Thurman had questioned him about which school he had attended, and Keith had named a school in Fort Myers. He wondered if Thurman suspected he was not really from Florida, but he refused to dwell on this.

At the start of the voyage, Lieutenant Savela had made known to the ship's captain how many members of the merchant crew he required as ammunition passers, and Keith's loader was Lincoln Johnson, the younger of two black steward's mates. Lincoln participated enthusiastically in training sessions and was always among the first at his post when the alarm sounded for gun drills.

One day as they were finishing a drill, Lincoln revealed to Keith that he had problems with some of the other galley crew, who drank heavily. This came as no surprise to Keith. On two occasions he had been served dinner by a drunk messman.

Lincoln also confided, "I want to be a navy gunner, but I'm the wrong colour. Negroes don't get to be anything better than stewards."

Keith knew that what Lincoln said was true, so all he could say in response was, "That will change one day. And you'll be ready."

As Lincoln wandered off, Keith looked up to see Thurman observing him. He could have sworn that Thurman mouthed the words "nigger lover".

The following day Keith and the other gunners were in the mess, and Lincoln was serving them their evening meal. Lincoln made the mistake of reaching in front of Thurman to hand Keith his plate of hot beans and gravy. At the same moment the ship gave a slight roll and Thurman thrust forward with his arm, sending the plate clattering along the table and spraying its contents. Thurman pushed himself to his feet and stamped out.

Lincoln looked downcast, and Keith helped him clear up the sticky clutter

There was another incident in the mess a few days later, one that did not directly involve Keith. He was reading a book, and Cormac Denehy, a big, strong former trucker who led the team on the five-inch gun, was seated beside him writing a letter to his sister. Thurman was at another table drinking a cup of coffee.

Emerson Simpson, the youngest member of the gun crew, wandered into the mess with his friend Postolski. Noticing Thurman, he squared his shoulders and approached him, saying in a nervous voice, "We'd like our cards back."

Thurman cupped his ear. "Didn't hear that."

Emerson repeated the request, his voice quavering. "We'd like our cards back."

Thurman drew deeply on his cigarette and exhaled, sending a cloud of smoke in Emerson's direction. "You know, it pisses me off to be interrupted when I'm having a quiet smoke." He put the cigarette down, glaring at Emerson. Then he addressed Postolski. "What's he trying to tell me?"

"W-w-w …"

Thurman sniggered, and waited.

"W-w-w …"

Thurman made a jerking motion with his hand in time with the stuttering.

Postolski persevered. "W-w-we know you've got them."

"You know I've got what?"

"We just told you." Emerson had suddenly found his voice. "Our playing cards."

Thurman rose from his seat, slow and deliberate. He loomed over Emerson and Postolski. "Oh, you mean those cards? The ones with the topless broads?" The other two said nothing, and he continued, his voice loud and sneering. "Only chance you'll ever get to fondle some titties, isn't it? Unless it's with each other."

Emerson's face reddened and he clenched his fist.

At that point Denehy called out, "It wasn't Thurman. It was Johanssen and me." He walked over and placed his hand on Emerson's shoulder. "Sorry, kid. Couldn't resist the temptation. Haven't seen any decent tits for weeks."

Emerson turned to him, clearly upset.

"Come on, the cards are in our quarters," Denehy said.

It was a quiet trip to the Persian Gulf, and Morocco was new to Keith. There was nothing to stir up troubling memories of the past. At Casablanca, the Armed Guard were given shore leave, half the men at a time. Keith and Steve Allison, his closest friend on the *Harold Beacon*, went ashore in the afternoon, pristine in their dress whites. Steve was a navy signalman whose role was to send communications, using a signal lamp, between the ships of the convoy. He had been married for one year and was a keen sportsman.

The port area was hot and shabby and smelt of urine, and there were spitting camels amid the crush of people. Bearded Arabs wearing turbans and long, flowing robes approached the two men with fistfuls of dollars, asking in broken English if they had anything to sell from the ship—cigarettes? sheets? American clothes?

Keith and Steve came to a halt, temporarily overwhelmed by the assault on their senses.

Steve motioned across at Thurman, who had disembarked before them and was standing nearby. "He doesn't like you much, does he? I've observed the way he is with you. Had the two of you met before?"

"Never met him in my life before this trip."

"Well, watch your back. One of the guys was on another ship with him, and he said Thurman gets even meaner once he has a few drinks inside him."

"Hmm. I think he resents Savela putting me in charge of the Oerlikons. Thurman believes the job should be his."

"It's yours by right. You're the one with two stripes on your shoulder, not Thurman. But he does look like he's used to getting whatever he wants. I think he's got a rich daddy. It's a wonder he didn't manage to wriggle out of war service."

"Perhaps his daddy thought it would make a man of him? Or maybe Thurman's running away from something? Or he could be doing it by choice. He likes the guns."

"You're very mature, pal, for one so young."

Keith shrugged. "Let's stop talking about Thurman. Anything particular you want to do this afternoon?"

"Shall we do some shopping first? My wife turns twenty-one in a few weeks and I want to buy a piece of jewellery for her. One of the engineers who's been to Casablanca before told me where to go. And you need a wristwatch, don't you?"

"Sure. Let's do it," Keith said.

Steve led him on a long, hot hike to an area of arcaded streets. The winding whitewashed walls were festooned with colourful robes hung on hooks, and there were little shops selling perfumes, leather bags, brass work and carpets. In another life Keith had been to such an area with Sergeant MacFarlane and Jimmy in Cairo. He thought back to that day and realised that at last he was able to bring to mind the *good* times he had shared with Jimmy.

The Arab quarter of Casablanca had antique shops, and Keith and Steve stepped through a curtain into one of these. It was cool inside with a humming fan, and the proprietor, smiling in a fez and white robes, brought them chairs and glasses of sweet mint tea. An hour later they emerged, Steve with an antique bracelet, Keith with a wristwatch and a silver and tortoiseshell comb. The last time he had shopped for anything that was not spartan and utilitarian, was the day he met Barbara in New York City. He preferred his life as it was now.

Back at the ship, they put on their swimming trunks and, laughing and high-spirited, played a game of volleyball. Then they doused each other with buckets of salt water to cool down.

The *Harold Beacon* had left the Mediterranean, on its voyage back to New York, and was in convoy off the French coast when in the middle of the night Keith was aroused from a deep sleep by strident, repetitive blasts from the ship's siren. He rolled out of his bunk, then shook awake two gunners who had slept right through the racket.

"General quarters!" he yelled.

He buckled his belt, pulled on a sweater, and joined the stream of men running to their action stations.

Lincoln was already at the gun, his shoelaces untied and his shirttails hanging out. His hands trembled as he tried to attach a magazine to the top of the breech casing. This was the first time it was not a drill.

Keith shouted to him, "Take it easy, pal. You know what to do." He jumped into the gun tub and strapped himself in. He slammed the barrel down to cock it.

There was the loud sound of an engine as a plane emerged from the clouds, flying low. Keith could see the swastika painted on its side as it swooped between the convoy columns. The men at the guns started chattering nervously.

Lieutenant Savela called from his action station on the bridge, "Wait for my order!"

Repeatedly on this voyage, during lectures on gunfire controls, he had stressed the need for discipline and targeted fire. He had cited incidents of inexperienced gunners who had holed deck cargo and fired at friendly planes.

The men waited. More planes approached. Junkers torpedo bombers. They dropped flares that lit up the darkness, and the convoy's escort ships sent up tracer fire, long streamers of light criss-crossing the sky.

"It's like the fourth of July," one of the men muttered.

"Fire!"

For the next hour it was bedlam, with men shouting, ships' sirens shrieking, machine guns clattering, bombs bursting with deafening thuds and anti-aircraft shells exploding like express trains passing overhead. Every now and then, a burst of flame shot from one of the bigger-calibre guns of the warships accompanying the convoy. On the shore there were pinpricks of fire; and out on the edge of the convoy a ship blazed. There was a smell of cordite in the air.

Lincoln had settled to his task and kept Keith supplied with fresh rounds of ammunition. The Oerlikon had a sixty-round magazine that fired at a rate of 450 a minute, so both men were soon sweating with the exertion. It all came naturally to Keith. He felt as if he were home again.

The Junkers bombers appeared to withdraw, and then one roared in close by on the port side. The guns on the *Harold Beacon* and the neighbouring ships all fired. Suddenly there was a large object burning above them and falling through the skies, circling down.

Excited voices shouted, "We got one. She's falling right here."

In a ball of flames, the German plane plunged into the sea.

It gradually quietened down after that, but for the next few days Keith and the other gunners stood watch around the clock, two hours on and two hours off. They would climb out of their gun tubs and lie down to sleep, and the next moment a buddy would be shaking them awake to start watch all over again.

Chapter 20

Adirondack Mountains, New York
July 1944

Keith was given leave following the voyage to the Persian Gulf
and he immediately contacted Vi and Art. They were about to set
off for their summer camp in the Adirondacks, their last visit
before autumn, so they invited him to join them.

Art had told him about the Adirondacks, the region of
mountains, lakes and bush sprawling across the middle of New
York State, isolated and bitterly inhospitable in winter but cool
and welcoming in summer, a refuge from the sticky heat of the
cities and towns of the north-east.

Their camp was one of half a dozen that nestled in clearings
on the point of a tree-covered spit that ran down the centre of a
long lake. Each camp was separate and self-contained, but the
people who lived in them formed a close-knit community who
came every year, some for a few weeks, others for the whole
summer. They socialised together and never locked their doors. It
was a world of its own, bypassed by highways and railways; the
only means of access was by boat.

Vi and Art's wooden cabin had a living room and kitchen
downstairs, bedrooms above, and a sleeping porch enclosed with
netting out in front. Vi said it lacked some of the comforts of
their city house. They used paraffin lamps, an oil stove and an
open grate in place of electricity. But that made it all the more
pleasant. It was summer, after all.

The house stood near the crest of a ridge, almost hidden

among the trees. On one side, a path led down to a boat shed and a landing; on the other side, the path descended to a gap in the trees and a low bank that spilled on to a small bathing beach. A diving raft made from oil drums lashed together with a wooden platform on top floated about thirty yards offshore. The water in the lake was clear except for patches of lilies drifting back and forth.

The first night, the three of them sat on the porch, Keith and Art with a whiskey in their hands, and Vi a vermouth. Keith breathed in deeply, inhaling the scents of nature: earth, leaf mulch, new growth.

Vi smiled at him. "You look as if you feel good about yourself."

Keith nodded. "The ghosts don't visit me in the dark any more."

"You look good in that new uniform too," Art said. "And you know it."

Keith laughed. "I enjoy being back in uniform, and I'm picking up more American ways. I still don't like Coca-Cola, though. I can't understand what the others see in it."

"Well, I have to admit, I'm not a fan either," Art said.

"Did you get my letters?" Vi asked.

"I didn't hear from you for a long time, then two letters arrived at once. Your letters have meant a lot to me. I've had to cut myself off from my friends at home."

"At least my letters reached you eventually. By the way, do you ever hear from the girl in New York?"

"Barbara. She sent one letter, to say she's going to marry a marine. I'm pleased for her. She's a nice girl."

"Remember my nephew, whom I told you about?" Vi said. "The one who joined the Merchant Navy?"

Keith nodded. "Elwyn."

"Well, he's just completed his first voyage, to England, and there was a Naval Armed Guard unit on board. He said the navy boys don't get paid as much as they do, so they shared their war risk bonus with them at the end of the voyage."

"Aye," Keith said. "They did the same on our voyage. Decent

of them. I believe it's the custom. We all rely on each other when we're at sea."

Vi excused herself, returning a few minutes later with a large envelope. "I'm sorry to spoil the mood," she said, "but I think I've got some bad news for you." She drew a newspaper clipping out of the envelope and handed it to Keith.

Keith looked at the clipping, and a familiar face jumped out at him. Spectacles and fair, thinning hair. Walter Simon. He caught his breath as he read the headline next to the picture: AMERICAN JOURNALIST KILLED BY V-1 FLYING BOMB.

"I go to the public library a couple times a week," Art said, "and I scan through the major New York dailies. This headline caught my eye because Vi has relatives in England."

"Is Walter the journalist you told us about, the one who gave you a ride to New York City?" Vi asked.

Keith nodded, as he began reading the article.

LONDON, AUGUST 7, 1944. American war correspondent Walter Simon was one of eleven people killed when a V-1 flying bomb struck south of London yesterday. The house where Mr Simon, 28, was staying received a direct hit from the robot bomb launched from Northern France. Of the six people in the house, only a young child survived.

Walter Simon had been based at the London bureau of the New York Times since September 1943. A fluent speaker of French and German, he reported on the D-Day landings, and then followed the advance of the Allies, filing stories from liberated towns in France...

He read the article to the end before he spoke again. "I've always looked on Walter as my first friend in America, even though we only met the once. I feel stunned that he's gone so soon."

Art nodded. "It's sometimes the way things happen. People die in a totally unexpected way."

"You must be upset," Vi said.

"I don't know if that's quite the right word. There are a few things I need to mull over in my mind later. I'll be all right."

"We understand, son," Art said. He looked at Keith and Vi. "I'd like to propose a toast to a clever and courageous man, with our thanks and respect." He raised his glass. "To Walter Simon."

"To Walter Simon."

That night, as Keith lay in a swinging bunk on the porch, he thought about Walter Simon. Their journey together along Highway 9 had been followed by the excitement of his first week in New York City. Was he regretful he had not taken up Walter on his offer to have a drink together? Yes and no. That one car ride, and their long conversation, was packed with meaning, and he would remember it always.

It was Keith's second morning in the Adirondacks. He was ambling along the path on top of the ridge with a tin in his hand, collecting blueberries for Vi to make a pie. The berries grew abundantly among the fern undergrowth. As he turned a corner and passed by the trunk of a large tree, he felt something brush lightly over his shoulders and tighten round him. Suddenly his arms were gripped to his sides by a rope and he heard a *whoop* from above.

He dropped to the ground, pulling the rope with him, and someone tumbled down on to him. Loosening his arms, he grabbed hold of his opponent. To his surprise it was a girl of about seventeen, clad in shorts, who twisted and struggled. He released her and leaned back against the tree.

The girl sat up, catching her breath, rubbing her elbows and brushing her hair from her eyes. Her skin was smooth and tanned. At last she spoke.

"I'm sorry. That was meant for someone else. When I saw it was you, I got such a surprise that I lost my balance. Otherwise you wouldn't have escaped so easily."

"Really?"

She scrambled to her feet, laughing. "That look on your face when I pulled the rope. It was so funny."

Keith laughed too. "When I grabbed hold of you, I thought you were a boy. Who did you think I was?"

"My younger brother."

"Are you usually so … athletic?"

"Oh, yes."

"All right. Now that you've knocked me over and tried to tie me up, how about helping me pick some berries?"

"Sure. My name's Diane."

Over the following days they became inseparable. Diane knew every trail around the lake and never tired of showing them to him. Usually she strode ahead, pausing at intervals for him to catch up. She would be barely out of breath, just a pink tinge to her cheeks, and with her hair tumbling down into her eyes. In the water she was fearless. She would dive in from the raft and twist her body around, remaining under the surface until he called out for her. She would surface in an unexpected spot, holding out her hand to him, and his heart would leap. And then she would challenge him to a race across to the other side of the lake.

They also paddled far up the lake in the canoe. Often they nosed along the banks and swamps hunting for bullfrogs. They rested the paddles and drifted slowly in, watching carefully. Diane was usually the first to spot a frog. She would warn Keith to keep the canoe steady, then she would take the fishing rod and lean far forward. The cord would be wound in, so the hook, with a piece of red flannel attached, was close to the end of the rod. She would slide in from behind or from the side, slowly dangling it in front of the frog. The red would anger the frog and it would snap at the flannel, Diane would give the rod a quick flick, and the hook would catch him it the fleshy part of its throat. A smooth swing of the rod and the frog was aboard. A quick knock on the head, then the back legs were severed and skinned. As the morning passed, the jar containing the freshly-skinned frog legs would steadily fill. They would make a delicious meal fried in batter later in the day.

One evening after dark, Keith and Diane took Art's

phonograph and a pile of records and rowed out on the lake in the cedar guide boat. The moon glimmered high in the sky and lights from the camp sparkled across the water. As they drifted, knees touching, oars now and then breaking the stillness, they listened to the soft swing music, and Keith wished there were no war, or anything to tear him away from here.

On the last day of his leave, Keith and Diane took the canoe and paddled far up the lake accompanied by Vi and Art in the guide boat. It was calm, with no wind to rough the surface, and the sun was not too hot yet. When they reached a sheltered cove near the top end of the lake, they paddled inshore and beached the boats, unloaded the basket and Art's fishing gear and gathered wood for a fire.

High up on the neighbouring hill sat an observation tower from which careful watch could be kept over miles of unscarred forest. Before lunch, Keith and Diane set out to climb up to it. They scrambled up the tangled slope behind the cove, picking their way through creeping vines that twisted round the rocks, and prickly bushes that clutched at their clothes and tore at exposed skin. When they reached the foot of the square tower, they rested to regain their breath, then began to ascend the flights of steps that wound round the sides. The ground was soon far below. There were gaping spaces between the supporting beams, so Keith kept his eyes firmly on the steps in front of him.

At last they climbed up a short vertical ladder that led through a trapdoor to an enclosed platform at the top. On all four sides they had a view of the lake, the forest and mountains, and a chain of lakes that stretched far away towards the horizon.

For a long time they stood there and watched. The sun broke clear of its cloud cover, and in the distance a thin trail of smoke, most likely from one of the camps, rose steadily. There was deep silence. No bird sounds. No wind to shake and bend the trees.

As Keith's arm tightened around the girl by his side, his mind drifted away. The distant peaks crept closer and grew flinty and rugged. The bush faded away and lost some of its greenness. The lake below—or was it the loch?—grew ever more still until it became a mirror, reflecting in its face a stone cottage. His feet stood not on the wooden platform but on a rocky crag overlooking the loch. The girl nestled her head against his shoulder and spoke slowly and softly. He could not quite catch what she said, but he would know that voice anywhere. His lips framed her name. Jeanne.

Then a hand gently shook his shoulder, and another familiar voice, a voice brimming with energy, said, "Wake up, Keith! You're miles away."

Keith started and his eyes widened. The stone cottage disappeared, the bush grew green again and the mountains receded. "I'm sorry. It's so tranquil here."

"Yes, and we've had such fun the last few days, haven't we? It's a pity you're leaving tomorrow."

He was about to make a light comment in response when Diane sniffed the air and said, "I'm sure I smell coffee. Let's go!"

As he waited for her to manoeuvre herself through the trapdoor, he gazed at the lakes below, but he was unable to recapture the scene of a few moments before. He turned, slid through the trapdoor and descended the steps after her. They clambered down the slope to the edge of the lake, and soon they saw smoke rising from the fire and Art waving to them. Diane raced ahead. Keith followed her slowly. How foolish he had been to think he could start a new life without acknowledging the hold his past had on him. He was suddenly overcome with the desire to return to Scotland—not to stay, just to see the land one last time

And to speak to the girl to whom he owed an explanation.

Chapter 21

Glasgow
September 1944

Keith returned to Scotland sooner than he had anticipated.

Not long after his leave in the Adirondacks, the *Harold Beacon* departed for the United Kingdom in a convoy of ships bound for Liverpool, Hull, Cardiff, Oban and Glasgow. They entered the Irish Sea from the south through St George's Channel and ran into a violent storm with gale-force winds. Her rudder damaged, the *Harold Beacon* limped across to the Clyde estuary, where tugs arrived to take her to Greenock.

As they moved slowly up the Clyde in a thick, cold mist, the men cursed but Keith smiled. He knew it well. The channel narrowed and the mist thinned, and they glided past grey stone buildings interspersed with green fields. A sunken ship showed only its masts and funnel. Further on, busy shipyards echoed and re-echoed to the clang of steel. A ferry laden with workers nosed its way across their bows, then the *Harold Beacon* moved to the side of the channel and berthed alongside the quay. Stocky figures in tweed caps and polo-necked jerseys or grimy oilskins stood in the sheds on the quayside, waiting for the drizzle to stop. Glasgow, sprawling along the river, looked dirty and grey.

Lieutenant Savela had promised the Armed Guard a few days' shore leave. They gave each other haircuts and talked enthusiastically about visiting Glasgow. Keith had mixed feelings. He was nearing home at last; but he was approaching danger as well, the danger of recognition.

The group of them, high-spirited and exuberant, took the bus into the city. Most of the others were going to the Red Cross Club in Sauchiehall Street, but Keith gave them the slip and headed towards the Buchanan Street Railway Station.

He was walking along Hope Street, when he felt a tap on his shoulder. His heart hammered in his chest, and in a flash he was back in New York City. But the person who addressed him was not a military policeman; it was Denis Thurman.

"I'm not interested in the Red Cross Club either," Thurman said. "I've visited Glasgow before, and I know more exciting places to have a drink. We can do the rounds together."

"No, thanks. I've got other plans." Keith said.

"Where are you going in such a hurry?" Thurman asked.

"None of your business."

"You come from around here, don't you?"

"No, I don't. I come from Florida."

Thurman gave a short laugh. "The others might believe that, but I don't. I'm the one from Florida. You're hiding something, Anderson, and I'm going to find out what it is."

Keith glanced at his watch. He needed to get to the station. "You're starting to get monotonous. Go away and enjoy your bars, and I'll carry on with what I want to do."

Thurman grabbed him roughly by the collar. "What's your dirty little secret?"

There was no time for anything else but instinct. Keith had a train to catch. He delivered a neat uppercut to Thurman's jaw, causing him to reel in surprise. Then he walked swiftly round the corner into Renfrew Street and along Port Dundas Road to the station.

He did not regret punching Thurman. He had asked for it. He knew there would be consequences, but he banished these from his mind.

He bought a third-class return ticket and boarded the train that waited at the platform. It would take him across the country and north to Inverness, where he would change trains again. As he travelled away from Glasgow, the mist and drizzle lifted, a good omen for his return home.

He stayed the night in Inverness and the next morning stepped out of his hotel into a clear day with just a few wisps of high cloud in the sky. The air was bracing, and the recent rain had freshened the landscape. As he resumed his journey, Keith's heart began to pulse with a strange beat. He would see home, and he would see Jeanne. But would she understand why he had done what he had done? And as for his father, Keith did not even know where he was.

As the train travelled west the landscape grew more rugged, but on this sunny autumn day the harshness was softened by splashes of colour. Shades of brown ranged from the fawn of the pasture fields near the railway line to the rust of the bracken- and heather-clad hills. The rock outcrops were a smooth grey, the jagged peaks beyond the hills emanated a gentle purple, and the birch trees scattered alongside streams that rushed to join a loch or a shingle river were turning yellow. When the line bordered one of these rocky streams, Keith would press his face against the window and strain to spot trout in the clear waters.

Occasionally they passed a grey stone house with a slate roof and narrow windows. There would be a potato field nearby, and a small round haystack with a pointed top, while further away, black-faced sheep grazed in a rough pasture.

At last, through the trees he glimpsed a larger stretch of water below in the valley. Soon the trees faded out and the line ran alongside a clear still loch that mirrored the landscape. Just as quickly the picture changed. Clouds moved into the sky; the sun peeped out between layers of stratocumulus and cast shafts of light and shadow that sparkled and shimmered across the surface of the loch.

Keith rushed from one side of the train to the other, gazing first through the window of his compartment and then through those in the corridor, anxious not to miss a single detail. He forgot the bitter cold and damp, the loneliness and isolation and the life of hard work and bare subsistence that drove most young people to the cities of the south or even overseas. His eyes moistened, and a wave of emotion rose deep in his stomach, coiled up and gripped his heart and surged into every vein until his whole body tingled. This was his homeland, and it had never been more beautiful than it was now.

It was Saturday, and Keith had booked into a hotel in a small town a few miles from the village of Lochcarron, where Jeanne lived and where he had been born. There had been limited contact between town and village when he was growing up, so he did not expect anyone here to recognise him; but locals would recognise his Scottish accent despite the Americanisms he'd picked up. He would avoid conversations with them as much as possible. His American uniform excited little curiosity. Most parts of the Highlands attracted service tourists.

The girl who showed him to his room and then turned back the bedcover and opened the window was too young to be suspicious of any slip of the tongue. He soon had her chatting about the district, and he steered the conversation around to the village.

"Oh, no," she said. "It's a wee bitty far to walk there. You'd need a bicycle."

"Will it be possible for me to hire one in town tomorrow?"

"Hire a bicycle on the Sabbath!" She pulled a face. "This is a ghost town on a Sunday. People hardly dare to move unless it's to go to church." She paused. "If you need a cycle tomorrow you can borrow mine. It's out in the yard there, against the far wall."

Keith smiled at her. He had noticed the ladies' bicycle through the window when he first came into the room. "Thank you. I'll accept your offer. Otherwise I'm stuck in a ghost town, aren't I?"

After dinner he stood at his window watching an enormous moon rise over the hills. He had planned everything carefully for tomorrow. He would go to the kirk by the lochside, arriving shortly before the end of the morning service. Jeanne would almost certainly be there, as most of the villagers, young and old, attended church on a Sunday.

He was aware he took a risk in visiting Lochcarron, but it was only slight. He had not been here in years. Most of his former classmates would be long gone and, in any event, no one would expect him to be in American uniform. He had written Jeanne a note in which he mentioned a special spot high above the loch that the two of them knew well, and he said he would wait there for her in the evening. He slipped the note into an envelope with "Jeanne" written on it, together with the brooch she had given him.

The sun was shining as he approached the kirk a short distance from the village. It was a simple stone building with lime-washed walls broken at regular intervals by tall, narrow windows. The V-shaped slate roof was topped at one end by what appeared to be a square box but which served as a bell tower.

The door was wide open and the voices of the congregation singing a psalm floated out. He had sung this psalm in the kirk when he was much younger, and as he listened his lips framed the words.

> *Lord, from the depths to Thee I cried.*
> *My voice, Lord, do Thou hear;*
> *Unto my supplication's voice*
> *Give an attentive ear.*

He moved closer. The singing had finished and they were saying the Lord's Prayer. Soon the minister would begin the sermon. *The sermons! They were interminable.* Keith smiled at the memory of the family that always sat in the pew in front of his. It included several small, wriggling children, and as soon as the sermon began the mother would hand a large round peppermint to each child, a special treat to keep them occupied.

He had not intended entering the kirk, but on an impulse he removed his cap and slipped quietly inside and took a seat near the door. In front of him stretched three rows of dark varnished pews, the backs of people's heads visible above. He thought he sighted Jeanne in the front row on the far side of the kirk, but he could not be certain. All the women and girls wore hats.

The interior of the kirk had barely changed since the days when he and his family attended. The walls were painted green to shoulder height and then cream up to the joint with the roof. Two brass kerosene lamps with shiny polished globes and white china shades were suspended over the aisles by long wires attached to the solid wooden cross-beams above . There was a thin railing in front of the pews, and beyond this, dominating the kirk, stood the pulpit.

The minister giving the sermon was a short, stocky man with a round, owlish face and glasses, who wore a black academic gown that seemed to swallow him up. He was a visiting minister, with an accent that was a soft mix of Scottish and American. He said he had once had a kirk in New York City. His delivery was plain and blunt, and he addressed the congregation directly without notes. From time to time, he gripped the sides of the pulpit with his hands, leaning forward as if to engage more closely with them. His preaching was based on a verse from Isaiah. *Look unto me, and be ye saved, all the ends of the earth.* The orientation was subtly different to the sermons Keith recalled from his childhood, which sometimes included descriptions of hell that frightened him and later alienated him. Instead, the minister asked the congregation to consider the universality of Christ's outlook.

"Christ's mission was worldwide in its scope, a mission for all the ends of the earth," the minister said. "There was no narrowness in the heart or in the purpose of Christ. The barriers and distinctions that divided nations and families and individuals from each other, creating misunderstanding and prejudice, hatred and strife, carried no weight with him. Although he was born in a Jewish household, he received the Syrophoenician woman, he welcomed the Greeks who sought to make his acquaintance, he rejoiced in the faith of the Roman centurion, and he spoke of other sheep not yet in the fold."

Near the end of his sermon the minister mentioned the young men from the area who were serving their country.

Little does he know, Keith said to himself, *that the sailor in American uniform sitting at the back of the church used to live round here.*

The minister paused for a moment, then went on to say, "The tide has turned. We are on a rising crest of victory, and soon we will have a chance to reshape the world and make it better than we have known it. We must cease to think of ourselves merely as nations, and consider instead a wider world, a wider people. Patriotism is a good thing, but it can also be evil when coupled with prejudice against race, colour or religion that differs from one's own."

He and Art should get together, Keith thought. But he wondered how the congregation would react to the minister's words. People around here were so conservative.

The minister continued, "We cannot hope to change the world unless we change human nature. To do this in our generation will be difficult, even impossible. But we can make a start through the education of our children—the children here in the village, in every part of this land and in every land on this globe—because they are the citizens of tomorrow."

The minister concluded the sermon and they sang the final hymn. As soon as the minister had given the benediction, Keith picked up his cap from the chair beside him and slipped out of the kirk and waited in the grounds.

Shortly afterwards, several people emerged from the kirk in a group. He recognised Jeanne among them, talking to a young man. Keith watched the two of them stroll along the path and stop by the stone wall that faced the road. The young man stood in front of Jeanne, feet planted firmly on the ground. He gazed down at her face, explaining something, and the two seemed intent on each other. Now they were laughing.

Keith told himself he had been foolish to come. Too much time had elapsed.

He was about to turn on his heel and leave, when the young man nodded to Jeanne and walked back to the kirk. This was his opportunity. But he hesitated. She might not recognise him. Certainly his strange uniform would confuse her.

She leaned against the wall and removed her hat. Now he

could see her hair, dark brown with lighter strands that glistened in the sun. She still wore it parted on the left, swept slightly from her forehead and tucked behind her ears, but it was cut shorter than before. And she was taller than he remembered.

It was now or never. Before he lost all his courage or the young man returned.

He walked right up to her, and she acknowledged him with a rather uncertain smile. He drew the envelope from his pocket, saying in a voice that seemed not to be his, "Could I ask you to ensure this reaches the right person, please?"

She took the envelope, read the name written on it and gave a start. She looked up again, searching his face. Slowly her eyes brightened. "Keith?"

He nodded.

The group who had been talking to the minister at the church door broke up and started walking along the path. One or two glanced at him. It was time to go.

He whispered to her, "Tonight."

Then, with a light touch of her arm, he turned and strode out the gate and down the road to where he had left the bicycle. He did not look back.

Chapter 22

Lochcarron
September 1944

Keith took a longer, little-known route to avoid being seen from the road. It was a steep climb, and he was panting by the time he reached the rocky outcrop that was his destination. He cut around to the front of the largest boulder, settled himself into the deep hollow at its base and waited. This was the perfect spot. He was hidden from the road far below but would detect anyone who approached.

Through the fronds of bracken he could see the sharp outline of the hills on the other side of the loch. They blazed purple and gold, caught by the sun, which hung low in the sky. There was a chill in the air and he was pleased to have his greatcoat. The heather, crushed beneath him, smelt pungent and earthy. He breathed deeply. This was the scent of home. He would carry it with him wherever he went.

Quiet and alert, he sat and listened. Nothing broke the silence except the distant calls of sheep and the chirping of a bird. After five or so minutes he spotted someone climbing up the hill below. As the person came closer, he saw it was a young woman, warmly clad in a tweed skirt, woollen jacket and a headscarf. Jeanne. He knew she would come.

She climbed steadily and was soon there in front of him, barely out of breath, with just a slight flush to her cheeks. Her skin was a soft natural brown. *Fithich dhubha Loch Carrann.* That's what the people of their village were called in the Gaelic. Black ravens of Lochcarron. He stood to face her, and she searched his face.

"It *is* you, Keith. When you gave me the note this morning I recognised your handwriting and the brooch, and it looked like you, but the uniform was all wrong. It's American, isn't it? What's happened?"

He laid his hand on her shoulder. "Jeanne. I'll tell you everything, but let's get you comfortable first." Squatting on his heels, he brushed the loose stones away so there was a smooth spot for sitting. They both sat down, he with his arm round her, and he felt her relax into his body. He told her what had happened since he last wrote to her from North Africa: the voyage across the Atlantic escorting prisoners with Joe McDonald, the fateful jaunt with Blue and Stretch, the desolate months in New York, his friendship with Vi and Art Spaulding. He explained why he was wearing this uniform, and told her that he was now known as Keith Anderson.

She listened in silence until he had finished, then she said, "The worst thing was not knowing."

"I'm sorry. I was ashamed, I suppose."

She nodded, saying no more about it, and he asked about his father.

"Your father is dead," she said.

He thought he should experience some emotion, but the news barely affected him. After his mother died, there had been little to keep his father and him together. He had visited his father occasionally, but they had never written to one another. It was like a friendship that had been drained of its lifeblood through neglect and lack of contact.

Jeanne continued. "He died not long after we received news that you were in hospital. The last word he had was from your platoon commander. He wrote and said you were recovering, and that you had conducted yourself in the true tradition of a Highland soldier."

"It would take more than that to impress my father."

She shook her head. "That's not true. He was proud of you. Very proud."

"Well, perhaps he had some feelings after all."

She frowned. "Of course he did."

"So he died before word came through about my desertion?"

Jeanne nodded. Then she said, "Your voice has changed a wee bitty. Like the minister who preached at the kirk this morning."

"I've picked up a twang. I've become half American." He pulled a comical face and pretended to slice himself down the middle. "But underneath, I'm still the boy you grew up with."

"You haven't asked about your aunt in Edinburgh."

"I've avoided thinking about her. She was good to me. She would have been upset to hear what I did."

"She doesn't know. Her health is failing and my father decided to protect her. She believes you're still somewhere with your unit."

"That was decent of him. It's probably the only time in his life he hasn't told the absolute truth."

Keith asked Jeanne about her sisters, and she said Chrissie was in Glasgow and Anna still at home. Then she told him about friends from his schooldays, but he felt remote from them. They belonged to another life. Why had he even come here?

He suddenly found himself saying, "Jeannie, we have to say goodbye. I'm leaving for Inverness tomorrow morning, and then to Glasgow. I'm due back at my ship on Tuesday."

He felt her body stiffen. She pulled away and turned to face him. "I despair of you, Keith. We're finally together again. You tell me what you've been doing for the past two years, I tell you about your father, and then all you say is farewell forever."

"But—"

"Keith. Do you feel anything for me?"

"You know I do. We grew up together."

"I mean now."

He said nothing.

"There's no one else, is there?"

He shook his head, "No one else."

"Then talk to me."

He said in a low voice, "I've never forgotten you, Jeanne. But for a long time, I've had to be guarded in everything I say. It's become a habit."

"If you can't say it, I will." Her gaze was direct. "I've loved you ever since I was a child. I still love you, and I'm not a child now."

"Aye. I'd noticed that."

Jeanne had unbuttoned her jacket, and he could see the outline of her breasts beneath her neat fitted jersey. Her face had matured too, but her expression was still innocent and unworldly, and he cautioned himself.

"Do you love me?" Her voice was firm and direct.

"Of course I do."

"Then we can take that as a starting point."

His smile was rueful. "There's not been much room for softness in my life recently. I live in a man's world. Even the married men don't talk much about their wives, although they keep their photos close." He struggled to express himself. "And, I have to admit it, I had an outdated picture of you in my mind. I still thought of you as a school girl." He lapsed into silence again.

"That was more than two years ago."

"The day we met up in Glasgow, before I went to Egypt. You'd just left school." He took her hand. "I can change too. Be patient with me."

She smiled at him, and he suddenly recalled something from the day before. "But what about the tall man who was talking to you after kirk yesterday? He found you attractive, I could tell."

"That's Donald. Aye, he's most attentive."

"Do you like him?"

She laughed. "You should see your face. I do like him, but only as a friend."

"After everything that's happened, you prefer me?"

"Believe it or not, I do. I've always been contrary."

"That's true. Remember the day you ran away in a huff, for hours in the cold, because you didn't like the way Anna had organised the household tasks?"

"And you searched until you found me, and brought me home wrapped in your coat. So chivalrous."

He rubbed his nose, reflecting. "That's part of the problem. I was brought up to believe a man should provide for a woman, and that means waiting until he can provide her with a home." He sighed heavily. "My future's so uncertain. It's unfair to expect you to wait for me."

"Who said I'll be waiting for you?"

"But I thought—"

"Oh, Keith. What's happened to your sense of humour?" She took his hand. "What I mean is, I won't just be waiting. I'm eighteen. I'm tired of the village. A few months ago I applied to the Glasgow Royal Infirmary to train as a nurse."

After allowing himself a moment to absorb the news, he said, "Nursing's a good idea."

"Oh, so I have your permission?"

He tried to explain himself. "You're full of surprises, Jeanne. I never imagined you leaving Lochcarron."

"How old am I?"

"Eighteen."

"How old were you when you joined the army?"

"Eighteen."

"And you were even younger than that when you left home."

He held up his hand. "I take your point."

She smiled with satisfaction.

He bent over and untied her headscarf. Then he brushed his face against her hair, breathing in the light scent of lavender.

She rested her head against his shoulder and her voice was slightly muffled as she spoke. "I went to Glasgow for an interview with the matron and I also sat an entrance exam. They've offered me a place at the Preliminary Training School. Thirteen weeks. Then if I pass the exams, I become a probationer in the wards. I start in two weeks' time." She raised her head. "Just think, we almost missed each other."

"That would have made me sad," he said, "to have travelled so far and then not see you. And I couldn't very well ask your parents where you were." He paused. "Your mother, how does she feel about you leaving home?"

"She got a shock when I first told her. Didn't say much at all, looked as if she was going to cry."

"I thought she'd take it hard. The two of you have always been close."

"I could hear her and Da talking after we went to bed that night. Anyway, at breakfast she said she'd give me her blessing."

"Glasgow's not far away. In time she might even become enthusiastic about it."

Jeanne laughed. "She's that already. She bought me a cabin trunk, and we're going shopping together. I have to buy two uniform dresses, three aprons and a hat, as well as cuffs and starched collars."

The hills on the other side of the loch had lost their colour and sat pencilled in silhouette against a pale sky. Jeanne shivered.

"You're cold. I'd better let you go home. They'll wonder what's happened to you."

"Aye, they will." She looked at him anxiously. "You'll come and visit me next time your ship's here, won't you?"

"Of course. I don't know when it will be. I go where I'm sent. But I won't neglect you again, I promise. You're too precious to lose. What's the address of the training school?"

"I'll be at 5 Lancaster Street. It's near the Botanic Gardens."

"I'll send you letters with the words all mixed up to tease the censors."

"Don't you get too clever or I won't understand what you're saying. Then I'll start writing in Gaelic, and you'll be the one having difficulties."

He laughed. "Aye, you're right. When you write to me," he added, "address the letters to Keith Anderson, US Navy." He looked at her, teasing. "Come on, you'll get used to it. Repeat it after me. Roll it around your tongue. Keith Anderson."

She said the words slowly and carefully. "Keith Anderson. Keith Anderson."

He reached into one of his inside pockets. "I have a wee gift for you. I bought it for myself, but I'd like you to have it." He drew out a slim silver case patterned with fine, swirling leaves, and he opened it up to show the tortoiseshell comb inside. "I bought it in Casablanca. Think of me strolling around in a sunny place, happy and relaxed. One day you and I will do that together." He folded up the comb and handed it to her.

He watched her as she put the comb in her pocket and began tying her scarf round her hair. "They must have noticed me talking to you at the kirk," he said. "Did they make any comment?"

"Aye. They said something about Yankee sailors chatting up the local lasses. I told them you were asking me how to get to Plockton."

He chuckled. "That would take me a while on a bicycle."

"So that's how you got here?"

"Aye. The lass at the Strathcarron Hotel loaned me her cycle for the day."

"Then we'd both better go. It will be dark for your ride back."

Keith rose and helped her to her feet. He put his arms inside her open jacket, wrapping them round her body. He held her close, inhaling her scent. She gave a deep sigh. He kissed her tenderly, and her lips were soft. They stood there for a long time and he could feel his heart pumping. Slowly, she drew away and began buttoning her jacket.

"I'll walk down the hill with you," he said.

"Just part of the way. We can't risk being seen together."

He accompanied her until she laid her hand on his shoulder and said, "No further."

He hugged her again, and then reluctantly released her. "*Beannachd leat.*"

"*Mar sin leat. Turas math dhut.* Safe journey."

He watched as she made her way down the hill, her figure getting smaller and smaller until she disappeared from view. Then he sat down and waited. The sky grew dark and a bright moon rose over the hills. Down below, pinpricks of light from the village were strung out sparsely along the near side of the loch. At last, sure-footed, he climbed down the hill, following the route that Jeanne had taken.

When he arrived back at the hotel, he went straight into the lounge. A fire burned in the grate, and on the table in the centre of the room there was a supper tray with a plate of food and a large brown teapot. He helped himself to a scone, some toast and a cup of strong tea, then took these to an armchair near the window. He was deep in thought and, apart from nodding to a couple seated near him, paid no attention to the others in the lounge.

Later, in his room, he wrote to Jeanne. It was a short and cautiously worded note, because he expected even more prying eyes in the village post office than in the censor's office.

Dear Miss MacKenzie,

Thank you for your kindness in talking to a visitor from America. I will soon be far away, but you can be assured I will not forget you.

With great confidence for the future,

Keith A.

Early next morning, he left the letter at the hotel to be posted before catching the train to Inverness, where he stayed the night.

Back in Glasgow the following evening, Keith stepped out of the Buchanan Street Railway Station, a plain low-slung wooden building fronted by a glass canopy that stretched over the wide footpath out front. People rushed by with their shoulders hunched up against the light driving rain. It was already dark, and the taxis drawing up in front of the station had their headlights in blackout mode, with louvres deflecting slim slits of light downwards to the ground. He set off, walking briskly, and had just turned into Sauchiehall Street when a familiar figure materialised in front of him.

"Well, look who's finally returned," Thurman said. "You and I have some unfinished business, haven't we?" His voice was slurred.

"After you've sobered up," Keith said. "A clean fight, fists, one-on-one."

Keith knew he owed Thurman a return bout. He had taken him unawares with his single punch four days earlier. But this was neither the time nor the place. Not only was Thurman drunk, but there was a good chance he had a knife hidden in his greatcoat. Before they went on shore leave, Lieutenant Savela had warned them to be prudent. Glasgow was known for street fights and the ready availability of knives (*and not to forget religion-fuelled fights in pubs*, Keith had thought to himself). And Thurman knew his way around.

"A clean fight?" Thurman sneered.

"Tomorrow, when you've sobered up. Meanwhile, there's a hotel across the street with good, cheap beds for the night. You can sleep it off there."

Thurman moved his hand towards his pocket, and Keith, realising that nothing could be resolved between the two of them here on the street, right now, made an instant decision. He leapt on to a passing tram, waited until it had rolled a block and then leapt off again. He glanced behind him. Thurman was nowhere to be seen.

He walked further along Sauchiehall Street to the Locarno Ballroom, where he spent an hour or two. Later in the evening he took his own advice and found a room in a quiet hotel.

By noon next day, all of the Naval Armed Guard were back on board. All except Thurman.

"Do you reckon he's run off?" Steve asked Keith.

"I don't think so. He more likely overslept. I saw him when I was heading back from the railway station, and he was drunk."

During the afternoon, Lieutenant Savela went ashore, serious-faced. It was four or five hours before he returned. That evening the Naval Armed Guard were summoned to the officers' mess. They crowded into the small room and stood between the tables, their eyes on Lieutenant Savela and the captain, who stood shoulder to shoulder. Both had grim expressions on their faces.

Lieutenant Savela cleared his throat. "A serious incident occurred last night. It involved Denis Thurman." He paused, and his eyes scanned the room. "Which of you saw Thurman last night?"

Three of the men confirmed they had been with Thurman in a pub early in the evening. They said he had stayed on after they left. He did not seem any different to usual and had not indicated his plans for the rest of the evening, other than drinking some more.

"Anyone else?"

Keith stepped forward. "I saw him on Sauchiehall Street at about half past eight. He was drunk, and I suggested he take a room at a hotel for the night and sleep it off."

"What happened next?"

"I went to the Locarno Ballroom for a while, and I spent the night at a private hotel."

"What about Thurman?"

"I don't know. I looked for him this morning in Sauchiehall Street, but I didn't see him."

After verifying that no one else had sighted Thurman, Lieutenant Savela glanced at the captain, who nodded. Then Savela turned to his men. "This afternoon I was at the police station in Glasgow. Thurman is being held in custody." The men broke into a babble of conversation, and Savela held up his hand. "At around ten p.m. he was involved in a fight in a pub. I understand it was racially motivated. He had a knife on him, and he stabbed another man, a civilian. This person is now fighting for his life in hospital."

The police questioned Keith and the others who had seen Thurman that night. Lieutenant Savela went into Glasgow several more times, and he gave the men brief updates on the situation.

"Thurman has been charged with a serious criminal offence. His father has been notified and is taking steps to find passage over here. The *Harold Beacon* will sail back to New York without Thurman."

Keith talked to Steve about aspects of his last interaction with Thurman, but he did not dwell on it, and he did not believe he could have acted differently. His hunch that Thurman was carrying a knife had proved to be correct. It was an unfortunate twist of fate that Thurman encountered someone who riled him even more than Keith did.

Chapter 23

Bari, Italy
October 1944

Keith was sitting at an outdoor table by the sea with other members of the Naval Armed Guard. This new voyage of the *Harold Beacon* had taken them to Bari, on the heel of Italy, and they had been granted a few days' shore leave at the port while the ship's cargo of assorted equipment and incendiary bombs was unloaded. They had spent the morning wandering along narrow paved streets, past whitewashed buildings adorned with iron balconies. Now they were enjoying a jug of robust local wine.

Lieutenant Savela joined the men, ordering more wine for them, and they chatted lazily in the sun, white caps pushed back on their heads. Keith was happy; everything was right with his world. He had received an affectionate letter from Jeanne, written before she left Lochcarron, and he was relaxing in the sun with a good team of men. With Thurman gone, there were no jarring notes.

Lincoln walked by with two other crew members. He waved at Keith.

"Lincoln's your greatest fan," Steve said.

Keith grinned. "He's very keen. He'd like to become a gunner." He watched as the three men conferred with each other, and then quickened their step. "I wonder where those three are off to?" His eyes roved around the group at the table as he quoted:

> *Said a certain sweet red-headed siren,*
> *"Young sailors are cute—I must try one!"*

She came home in the nude,
Stewed, screwed, and tattooed
With lewd pictures and verses from Byron.

Some of the men stared blankly, others sniggered or chuckled, and Denehy, after reflecting for a moment, leaned back in his chair and guffawed.

Emerson stared at Denehy. "What's Byron?"

"I have no idea," Denehy roared.

The whole group fell about laughing.

Keith was wondering if it was worth trying another limerick on them, when Alfred Caruso, master of the *Harold Beacon,* walked past with a purposeful step, nodding at the Armed Guard in his usual courtly manner. A small man, with a pronounced Sicilian accent, he had taken command of the ship just before this voyage to Italy. From the gossip that swirled around, Keith knew that Caruso had forty years' experience at sea, having served in the Italian Navy as a young man before immigrating to America and becoming a citizen, and he was widely respected by the merchant crew. He also understood that Caruso was not convinced of the need for naval gunners on merchant ships, at least not in a well-guarded convoy.

"I've never seen Caruso so relaxed," Keith commented to Steve. "He usually has a stern look on his face."

Steve, who worked closely with Captain Caruso in his role as a signalman, said, "He's on his way to visit relatives. He told me this is almost his last voyage, and he and his wife hope to retire to Italy after the war."

"Hmm. So that's why we came to Italy," Keith laughed. Then he turned to Savela. "Do you think you'll stay in the navy after the war ends, sir?"

"Most unlikely. I want to return to my job as a science teacher." Savela smiled. "I've got a wife at home and I've just heard we're expecting our first baby early next year."

"You were busy on your last leave, sir," one of the men said cheekily.

Lieutenant Savela laughed.

"Where's home for you, sir?" Steve asked.

"Hibbing, Minnesota. My parents immigrated there from Finland just before the First World War. My father's a Lutheran pastor."

"Finland. What's that?" Emerson gazed vacantly at the group. The glass of wine in the hot sun had gone straight to his head and his words were slurred.

"It's a country to the north of Europe," Keith explained. He glanced at Steve. They would need to keep an eye on Emerson. The previous night, he had got so drunk on a few glasses of wine that the shore patrol had asked them to deliver him back to the ship. They had lugged him down a hundred steps.

"What do you plan to do after the war, Keith?" one of the men asked.

Keith had no idea. He lived from day to day. And so he said the first thing that entered his head. "Dunno. Open a garage, maybe."

Steve chortled. "What prompted that? You've never expressed the remotest interest in cars."

Keith suddenly felt cornered, and he was trying to work out what to say next when one of the others intervened. "If you want to open a garage, talk to Don Franklin. He's going to retire from the Merchant Marine soon and buy a gas station near Boston so he can put his two nephews through college. He's a great guy." Don was the chief engineer on the *Harold Beacon*, one of the older officers on the ship.

The men soon dropped the subject of gas stations and started discussing their plans for the next day, which included local sightseeing and fishing from the wharf; however, the interchange had reminded Keith of the thin line he continued to tread in his new life.

After the voyage to Italy and the Adriatic Sea, the *Harold Beacon* underwent annual inspection by the United States Coast Guard at the Bethlehem shipyard in Boston. During this period Captain Caruso went to the shipping hall and hired merchant crew for the next voyage. The gun crew were given leave, and Keith spent several days with Vi and Art.

When he returned to the ship, he observed that welded steel reinforcement plates had been added along her sides. He commented on this to Steve, who shrugged his shoulders.

"Either the old tub's falling apart two years after she was built, or we're going somewhere with heavy seas."

They spoke no more of it at the time.

At the end of the week the *Harold Beacon* sailed up the coast as far as Halifax to pick up the rest of her cargo and her next assignment.

Chapter 24

Halifax, Nova Scotia
November 1944

Keith stood near the top of Citadel Hill, gazing down at the broad panorama of the city and harbour. Directly in front was the small mound of an island, and to the far right, guarding the entrance to the outer harbour, bulged a larger island. From his vantage point, it was cut in half by the spire of a cathedral. In front of him, the stream lay flat and calm, and he could see a ferry chugging across to the other side and two merchantmen steaming slowly towards the far left. They would be making for the Narrows and beyond that the Bedford Basin, where a convoy would assemble. His own ship was tied up at the wharves loading its cargo, so he had been given a few hours' leave.

It was almost the last day of November and the cold nipped at his ears, but the air was clear, with some weak sunshine and none of Halifax's notorious fog. He breathed in the clean scent of spruce and reflected on the day eighteen months earlier when he had first visited Halifax, when he had been naively uninterested in the city.

He picked his way down one of the rough paths towards the city. There was no snow as yet and a few brave dandelions poked up their heads from the balding grass slope. A soldier and a girl snuggled under the young man's greatcoat, and Keith thought of Jeanne.

As he continued down past the old clock tower, his view of the harbour narrowed to a slice between the solid old buildings lining Carmichael Street. He crossed the Grand Parade, continuing on to Barrington Street, the main thoroughfare. It was late morning and a sprinkling of people were out walking: a group of French sailors, a businessman with a briefcase, two well-dressed matrons, and an elderly man wearing a tam-o'-shanter. The man was parallel with Keith when he suddenly stumbled on the uneven footpath. In a reflex action Keith reached out and caught him before he fell.

"Thank ye, laddie," the man said in a trembling, barely audible Gaelic lilt.

Keith supported the man's elbow with his hand, as he appeared confused and shaken and in no condition to continue walking. "Let me take you in here for a cup of tea," he said, indicating the restaurant beside them. "I was about to have one myself."

The man brightened up immediately at this offer and, once Keith had helped him inside and they had settled themselves at a table, he became very talkative. He introduced himself as Hamish Munro and said his family had immigrated to Nova Scotia from Scotland sixty years ago.

Keith observed his wiry frame, his tanned wizened face and his alert blue eyes. "You're a seafaring man, aren't you?" he said.

"Aye, laddie. I spent my life in the merchant marine. I've been to Russia, Casablanca, India, Australia, New Zealand, right round the world." He talked to Keith about his adventures at sea and concluded by saying, "I'm land-bound now, but I watch the ships every day. Where are you off to?"

"I don't know. They never tell us until we're out at sea with the convoy," Keith said. "They've modified the ship, reinforced the sides with steel plates."

"You'll be going somewhere with violent seas." The old man began to look agitated. "I hope I'm proved wrong, laddie, but I think you're going up into the Arctic, through the Norwegian and Barents Seas, to Russia." He began fumbling at his neck. "Help me take this off, laddie."

Keith stepped round behind him and helped him remove a slim leather strap with a small pouch attached.

"I want you to put this round your neck, but let me show you what's inside first." With trembling hands Hamish opened the pouch to display its contents: a pale, wrinkled skin that was almost transparent. "I bought it from an old midwife in Halifax when I was a young sailor, after I nearly drowned." Keith frowned, and Hamish explained, "It's a caul. I carried it with me on every voyage. It's said to protect you against drowning. I'll never go to sea again, so it's yours now. You'll need it."

Keith thanked the old man and made to slip the pouch into his pocket.

"No. Put it round your neck. You have to wear it." While Keith hung the strap round his neck and tucked the pouch under his uniform, Hamish continued, "I fell into an ice cold sea once. When my head went under, I gasped. It's what you do naturally. But then I panicked and swallowed a lot of water. I was nearly dead when they fished me out. If you ever fall in, try to keep calm until your head's back above the surface." He rocked back and forth, his brow furrowed. "And always wear wool next to your skin," he concluded.

Promising he would not forget this advice, Keith glanced at his watch. "I'm sorry. I have to get back to my ship now. But you stay here and finish your cup of tea." He shook the old man's hand. Five minutes later he was down on Lower Water Street making his way towards the pier where his ship was berthed. The wind had changed, so it brought in the fog. The air was moist and smelt salty. Out on the stream a ship's engine thudded. He felt the caul against his chest and wondered if any of the seamen on the *Harold Beacon* had cauls. Some of the older men, in particular, were superstitious and carried rabbits' feet and other amulets.

When he got back to the pier, he noticed Jake Krakowski, the chief cook, watching crates being loaded into the *Harold Beacon*'s holds. The cook, a man of about forty with strong arms and a big belly, had joined the crew at the beginning of the voyage to Italy. Relations between Keith and him were strained. This stemmed from an episode on the Italian voyage when the gunners had been required to stay on duty well beyond the dinner hour, and, through an uncharacteristic lapse, no hot meal was kept for them. Keith had spoken up on behalf of the men and offended Krakowski.

Now Keith paused beside him and said awkwardly, "Looks like we'll be on our way soon."

The cook shook his head. "Captain isn't happy. Three of the crew he hired in Boston took off when they worked out where we were going. He's trying to find replacements now."

Keith wondered where Krakowski got his information from. "So where are we going?" he asked.

"Look at those crates. What do they mean to you?"

"Well, we're in Canada so I'd say cereal. Food for someone. And maybe heating equipment. Keep someone warm. And tanks. Transport."

The cook stared at him. His eyes were bloodshot. "Can't you read? What's written on the crates?"

Keith turned his attention to the crates. "Murmansk, USSR. Oh, so that's where we're going."

Krakowski gave a slow clap. "He's finally worked it out. So now what do those crates mean to you?"

Keith was becoming irritated. "Heavy seas, cold weather, and some action. We only got one good show on the Italian run."

The cook's face reddened. "You haven't got a clue, have you? The only thing you navy boys know is your guns." Krakowski gave him an unpleasant look. "You'll get your good show all right. In the shipping halls they call Murmansk 'the suicide run'. Those crates mean day after day without sleeping. They mean German torpedo bombers waiting for us all the way up the coast of Norway. They mean treacherous weather and monstrous seas. I've been there before. I know."

"Then I'm surprised you're going back."

Krakowski glared at him and then, unsteady on his feet, made his way up the gangplank.

Keith lingered on the pier a while longer, watching as a crated army tank was loaded into the hold. The cook was correct in that he did not know exactly what he was in for, but he hoped the apprenticeship he had served—rigorous navy training and his previous voyages—would be enough to prepare him.

By evening the Naval Armed Guard were all back on board, while those of the merchant crew who wished to make the most of their last night of liberty were still on shore—at a dance, drinking in a bar, or getting an extra kiss from a girl by telling her, "We're shipping out soon."

Keith and Denehy played some rounds of nickel-and-dime poker with two of the merchant boys. (They had been warned when they joined the *Harold Beacon*, "Don't play poker with the merchant crew. There's no way you'll win." But that did not stop them.)

Afterwards they chatted idly together, a group of about eight men. The destination for their forthcoming voyage had become an open secret. Rumours were circulating, hunches speculated on. Why else would they have installed extra heating? What about the white lettering stencilled on the crates?

Today was also the seventeenth birthday of Hopkins, the youngest member of crew, and the others teased him mercilessly, advising him, "Make the most of it, Hop. It'll probably be your last."

Emerson bounced into the mess. "There's a group of old dames on the pier, serenading us. Come and listen."

The men went out on to the deck and hung over the rails. Down below on the pier, a choir of about eight middle-aged women, snugly clad in woollen coats and hats, sang Christmas carols. They paused between each carol to receive the cheers and whistles of the assembled men, and sometimes during a carol they would call out, "Join in the chorus, boys."

When the singing had finished, one of the merchant officers went down to invite the women on board.

"It's a little early, but we know you boys will be away for Christmas," one of the women said. "So we've bought you some seasonal cheer."

The women proceeded to dispense ditty bags from baskets they carried. Each bag contained soap, toothpaste, toothbrush, razor—"Just in time for your first shave, Hop"—notepaper, pen and a handknitted item.

Afterwards the men sat around clad in their new parrot-coloured finery, fooling and joking, hands wagging in striped socks, gloves draped over their ears, scarves tied in bows under their chins.

Chapter 25

For three days they lay quietly at anchor in the Bedford Basin, as other merchant ships—British, French, Icelandic, and Dutch—joined them. The *Harold Beacon* had in her holds 7,500 tons of general cargo including heating equipment, farm machinery and construction equipment, as well as flour and cereal. On the upper deck, railway locomotives sat cradled in heavy twelve-by-twelve-inch beams. A wooden catwalk had been constructed along the port side so the gunners could dash back to the guns in the stern.

Captain Caruso, along with masters from the other ships, went to a pre-convoy conference at the port director's office, where he received his sealed instructions from the naval administration regarding the convoy destination. Then, the following day before dawn, the thirteen ships followed each other in line, along the Narrows to the stream and then out through the submarine net into the Atlantic. They moved slowly, each vessel keeping station three hundred yards behind the one immediately in front.

Out in the open sea, they made rendezvous with the large convoy that had departed from New York two days earlier. This convoy of sixty or so ships, already twelve columns across, slowed down so the ships joining from Halifax could form two new columns on the port side. The convoy sailed to the North-west Ocean Meeting Point off the coast of Newfoundland, where the local escort left them and a Canadian ocean escort of corvettes and destroyers arrived.

They turned eastward towards Great Britain, and once again Keith kept watch in a steady rotation with the other gunners.

Fore and aft of the *Harold Beacon*, and extending far to the starboard side in tight columns and rows, were other grey-hulled ships, low in the water, thrusting steadily forward, intent on keeping station in the convoy. Occasionally Keith saw the flutter of signal flags, or the flash of Aldis lamps at night, conveying course and speed changes ordered by the convoy commodore's ship. He would feel the slight change in the pulsation of the *Harold Beacon*'s engine, then he would blink his tired eyes and pass his tongue across his dry salty lips.

At the Mid-Ocean Meeting Point, escorts from the British Navy arrived to replace the Canadian escorts. As they crossed the Atlantic, the convoy was blessed with fair weather and moderate seas and, despite scattered reports of U-boats, there were no enemy strikes against the ships.

Keith stood on deck with the rain dripping down his oilskin coat and on to his sea boots. For the past five days the *Harold Beacon* had lain at anchor in Loch Ewe, a sea loch in the remote North West Highlands of Scotland, while a convoy—this time an Arctic convoy—assembled. It was early winter, and most days it rained, with a cold wind blowing in from the sea. Loch Ewe was ten miles long by four miles wide, and the merchant ships were in the lee of a large island that was flat at one end and rose to a peak at the other. The village of Poolewe was tucked away at the far end of the loch, hidden from view by a headland. The only sound, apart from the wind and the seagulls, was the *putt-putt*ing of a motor launch that had just departed with Captain Caruso and the chief radio operator on board, bound for the pre-convoy conference at Pool House Hotel.

Before coming out on deck, Keith had checked the winter clothing he had been issued: a sheep-lined Arctic coat, winter trousers (lined bibbed overalls), waterproof jackets and trousers, two winter helmets, a face mask, goggles, a winter sweater, a scarf, winter mittens, waterproof mittens, two sets of heavy underwear, six pairs of winter socks and a pair of sea boots with wool felt inner soles. Checking the clothing helped fill in some time. There was little to do while the ship waited here beyond reading and playing cards, as no shore leave was granted and no mail was collected.

The following morning the twenty-four merchant ships moved slowly out through the submarine boom, a barrier of light steel nets. When they reached the mouth of the loch, they turned northward and began to pitch and roll as the open sea met them. They were heading into U-boat-infested waters and were surrounded by a heavy naval escort with ASDIC underwater detection devices pinging and radars scanning the sea.

By the third day they had passed between the Faroes and the Shetlands, some four hundred miles east of Iceland. The weather had become markedly colder, and Keith was heavily wrapped up as he stood duty on deck. They were in U-boat territory again, so the escorts frequently dropped depth charges. The vibrations were unnerving, like sledgehammers pounding the *Harold Beacon*'s side, and she rose slightly in the water as each charge went off.

Two days later Keith was in the mess with a group of others when the raucous sound of the alarm bell began ringing in his ears. He flung on his Arctic coat, seized his steel helmet and kapok life jacket, and dashed out to his action station. Once in the gun box with Lincoln, who was barely recognisable beneath multiple layers of clothing, he finished dressing. He pulled his balaclava helmet from his pocket and put it on, retrieved a scarf from the same place and wound it round his neck, put the steel helmet over the balaclava and the life jacket over the coat and, lastly, slipped his hands into wool-lined mittens.

Overhead, just out of gunfire range, buzzed a single German aircraft. Keith examined it through his binoculars. It was a long-range reconnaissance plane, a Focke-Wulf Courier. It would be able to shadow the convoy for hours without refuelling, all the while sending radio signals to its base in Nazi-occupied Norway, information that could be used by bomber aircraft and submarines to attack the convoy.

The wind had ice in it, and Keith and Lincoln both became colder and colder as the plane went slowly around in wide circles above them. The beat of its engines came faintly across the water.

Lincoln's eyes followed the plane. "That pilot is spooking me. And he's making me dizzy. Does he always have to go in the same direction?"

"I never think about the pilot, just the plane," Keith said. "But someone told me a story about a ship's captain who signalled the pilot of one of these planes to ask if he'd mind circling in the opposite direction, and the pilot very courteously agreed. Shall I ask Steve to talk to Captain Caruso about signalling this pilot?"

"Good idea."

"Just kidding."

"I know."

"Captain Caruso wouldn't think it was funny."

"He would not. He's a stickler for the correct protocols. Yes, sir."

When the big plane finally left, it was not immediately replaced by another because the weather turned gloomy, with sleet and snow squalls and heavy seas running. It was unpleasant, but it meant they were safer. In such weather it was almost impossible for submarines to operate, and the low cloud and poor visibility made it difficult for the Germans to use their air reconnaissance to track the convoy.

As they headed northward they altered course a few points to starboard, following the approximate line of the Norwegian coast that lay some five hundred miles to the east. They could not see this coast, but its presence, dotted with German bases, was menacing.

The weather, although ever colder, cleared again; and one day an allied plane, a long-range Catalina, appeared overhead. It was a reassuring sight. Shortly afterwards, a flicker of Morse code came from the Catalina, followed by an urgent flutter of flags from the halyards of the ships. The convoy made an emergency turn in time to avoid the submarine that had suddenly surfaced. The escorts fired at it and it promptly submerged. Rumour was that they sunk it.

They were in the Arctic Circle now and had altered course

again so they headed east-north-east. It had become dim, never brighter than a semi-twilight. The ships steamed along close together, and the men were on alert continuously. They slept fitfully, fully clothed, and they each had a "scram bag" packed.

It was a still night, laden with frost, and Keith stood watch on deck. Beside him stood Lieutenant Savela, who was on his evening rounds. They both had their eyes lifted to the aurora borealis. It was as if a fire burned somewhere below the horizon, casting up cold flames of green and pink in a whirlwind across the dome of the sky. The aurora illuminated everything with a pale, unearthly light, and the other ships of the convoy stood out in black silhouette. It was hard to believe they were all moving steadily forward. They appeared motionless, suspended above the water.

Keith said in a quiet voice, "Day after day, day after day. We stuck, nor breath nor motion. As idle as a painted ship, upon a painted ocean."

"Poetry?" Savela asked.

"Samuel Taylor Coleridge. 'The Rime of the Ancient Mariner'. I learned it at school." Keith laughed at the memory. "Our teacher, Dribbling Willie. He had a loose lower lip, and when he got excited he'd spit, so we learned to stay out of the firing line. It's a pity he only stayed a year. I learned a lot from him." He stopped abruptly. This was the kind of night that invited confidences, but it was unwise to talk too much about his past. It might attract awkward questions.

Lieutenant Savela looked up at the sky again. "It's easy to believe in God when you are presented with a sight like this."

"Not God as an omnipotent creator," Keith said. "It's never easy to believe that, even when you're looking at the aurora borealis. But if you mean something awe-inspiring, bigger than us, something wonderful that we are part of—yes, that's easy to believe." He waited for Savela to agree or disagree, and when he said nothing, he added, "On the other hand, I'm half expecting to see a mythical creature."

Lieutenant Savela nodded. "In Finland the name for the aurora is *revontulet*. It means fox fires. My mother used to tell me a fable from the old country, about a magical fox who would sweep his tail across the snow, spraying it into the sky to form the fires." He turned to Keith. "Did your parents tell you stories?"

"My mother did. She was from Scotland and she used to talk about the lights. She called them *fir chlis*, the nimble men."

"That's apt. The lights do appear to dance," Savela said. "My mother also told me her own mother used to say that when the fires blazed in the sky children needed to be very quiet and respectful, because the fires came from the souls of those who had died." He chuckled. "She couldn't use that one with me, because in Michigan the aurora is rare."

"One day," Keith said, "you'll tell your own children about the magical fox that sweeps his tail across the snow and makes the sky light up with fire."

"One day, God willing."

On the tenth day, the convoy split. Some ships headed for Archangel on the White Sea, and the remainder prepared to enter the Kola inlet below Murmansk. A group of escorts went ahead of the merchant vessels, prepared to deal with the U-boats known to be ranging outside the entrance, where the merchant ships were at their most vulnerable, lining up to enter the harbour.

The *Harold Beacon* put down anchor partway along the stream, which was thirty-five miles in length, to wait her turn to be unloaded at the quays. Although the middle of the day, it was twilight. Keith looked across at the stark hills, and he sniffed the clear, crisp air. He knew that despite the discomfort and lack of sleep they had had a lucky run with not a man or a ship lost. It was almost too good to be true.

Chapter 26

Murmansk, Russia
January 1945

"Amerikansi. Slava Amerika!"

The crowd, mostly women, cheered and waved as the *Harold Beacon* steamed slowly to her berth. Two young women with dyed blonde hair waited among the unofficial welcoming committee, and one of them lifted her skirt provocatively. The seamen on the deck of the *Harold Beacon* whooped and started tossing packs of Camels and Chesterfields on to the rickety wooden quay, causing the women to scramble and fight in the snow for the cigarettes, which would fetch a fortune on the Murmansk black market. Thin, grim-faced prisoners toiled under guard among the cranes and railway wagons, piles of canned food, supplies yet to be processed from earlier convoys, and the smell of oil and rot. Noisy martial music played from loudspeakers.

The *Harold Beacon* remained in Murmansk for six weeks, throughout January 1945 and into February, with temperatures below freezing every day. The railway locomotives on her deck were unloaded by British crane ships, as Murmansk lacked facilities to unload heavy deck cargo; and Russian dockside cranes helped lift the loads out of the holds. Russian women, in bulky padded jackets and thick ankle boots, clumped on board to operate the winches.

The people of Murmansk had been through harsh times. After months of battering by Nazi bombers, all that remained of their town were scattered wooden huts interspersed with little groups of brick and concrete buildings. They regarded new arrivals with suspicion. The officials who boarded the *Harold Beacon* on her arrival read out a list of restrictions on what the men could bring ashore: no cameras, printed matter or weapons.

While the ship waited at the dock, the Naval Armed Guard were not all required on board, and so Lieutenant Savela allowed them ashore, half at a time. The rest of the time, when confined to ship, they had little to do other than exercise their guns every hour to prevent them freezing up. They would play cards until late at night and during the day sleep or listen to the radio. Sometimes they would fish over the rail for whitefish. Occasionally, they got a shotgun and competed to see who could shoot the most seagulls in one shot. The gulls were an easy target when lined up along the rail.

Keith wrote a letter to Jeanne in which he cautiously began to use words like "dearest" and "darling":

Dearest Jeanne,

How are you? I have been trying to imagine you in your new life.

I am very well. We are far north, in a cold place where you never see the sun at this time of year. Just a few hours twilight in the middle of the day before it becomes black night again. But despite the bleakness, everyone is pleased to feel firm ground under their feet. Our lieutenant, who is a fine skier, took a group of us to a nearby slope one day. My skiing is—how shall I put it?—workmanlike. But my buddy Steve is fast and graceful.

We have been bartering with the people of this place—cigarettes, soap and coffee for sleds, skis or other items made locally. (One of our fellows told me that a man tried to sell his wife to him for a few sweaters. Perhaps he exaggerated.) I managed to obtain a pretty woollen scarf for you. It is very fine and embroidered with bright flowers. I look at it sometimes and imagine it framing your lovely face.

I had intended to make this letter longer, but a big bag of mail has just been dumped on the deck. The merchant boys are jubilant and shouting, and have embarked on a flurry of letter writing.

Lieutenant Savela will go to the Navy HQ to check if the convoy brought any mail for us, and I will give him this letter to post. I hope it reaches you without too much being removed by the censor.

I would like to be able to tell you in person how much I love you and miss you. Perhaps you can sense it when I am thinking of you.

Bidh gaol agam ort fad mo bheatha, thusa 's gun duine eile,

Keith

Keith and Steve lingered inside the doorway of the Seamen's Club amid the smells of smoke, warm bodies and sweat and the sounds of stringed instruments being tuned, competing with the babble of voices. As Keith's eyes processed the room into individual figures, he spotted three seamen from the *Harold Beacon*. They stood with glasses in their hands, eyeing some Russian girls who sat lined up against the wall dressed in blouses, full skirts and heavy stockings. One of the girls looked familiar. Perhaps she operated a crane on the wharf. When the dance music started, the seamen made their way across to the women and girls on the opposite side of the room and began shuffling around the dance floor, awkward in their snow boots.

Steve prodded Keith in the back, saying, "Come on, pal. Let's get a drink."

The limit at the Seamen's Club was one drink of vodka, a generous one, with a glass of green tea for a chaser. After twenty minutes or so, fortified by the alcohol, Keith and Steve took to the dance floor. One of Keith's dance partners was an attractive blonde woman, full-figured and well groomed, who propelled him around the floor.

When the dance ended, as he escorted the young woman back to the wall, she touched his hand and said, "Would you like to come home with me?"

Keith was startled. Word was that after the last dance, the women would be herded into trucks for the return trip to their barracks. Was she suggesting he accompany them? Or perhaps she was amusing herself, imagining the reaction in her faraway hometown if she took an American sailor home with her. He politely declined: "I've got a girl in Scotland."

She looked at him knowingly. "She is there. I am here."

He shook his head, and they both laughed.

The men were absorbed in tossing the ball back and forth, and none of them noticed Keith approaching.

He called out, and Denehy looked up.

"What kept you, pal?"

"These three." Keith indicated the trio of youngsters behind him.

The littlest boy would have been six or seven years old; the oldest, already hard-faced, no more than twelve. They were obviously brothers—you could see the resemblance in their faces—and were far too lightly clad for the sub-zero temperatures.

"They sold me this for all the cigarettes I had on me. I thought we could use it tomorrow."

He put down the roughly hewn sled he had been carrying, and the two youngest boys promptly sat on it. He wondered if it, or they, would still be there when the game was over.

Denehy tossed him a glove. "You take centre field."

The Naval Armed Guard had prepared a baseball diamond on an area of hard snow beside the Murmansk Palace of Culture. Denehy and Steve had paced off the distances between bases and marked them with tin cans. Home plate was an old roasting dish cajoled from the galley staff.

Keith had first wielded a baseball bat several months earlier in Italy. Claiming to be rusty in his skills, he managed not to disgrace himself. From years of playing shinty, *camanachd*, in Scotland he was accustomed to the small, hard ball, though the rules of the two games had little in common and the shinty stick, with its two slanted faces and curved end, was completely different to the smooth, round baseball bat. His quick reflexes and ability to run fast helped too.

The American boys seemed obsessed with baseball, and it was the subject of numerous bull sessions on board ship. They talked about their favourite teams and players. Keith remembered Art talking about Joe DiMaggio of the New York Yankees, so he dropped DiMaggio's name into the conversation. The boys also reminisced about playing catch, hitting ground balls and practising batting with their fathers when they were kids. Denehy talked of baseball games on the street with the other boys back in Baltimore, and how they would repair the ball with black friction tape when the cover came off after constant use, and eventually it became so misshapen that they had to beg, borrow or steal another one.

Keith mostly kept mum during these sessions. How could he describe the summer evenings when he and Duncan batted balls for hours on a flat patch of ground near the cottage? His father had got them started by setting up two balls on a length of strong cord attached to metal stakes driven into the ground. Keith had gone on to play in a shinty team. He took left wing position, or right wing or centre ground.

When they played baseball in Italy, Emerson, to everyone's surprise, proved to be fast and nimble on the field. Afterwards he confided that his father had been a minor league baseball player who had put a baseball in Emerson's crib when he was a baby. And growing up he had read stories about a baseball player named Frank Merriwell in old *Tip Top Weekly* magazines from when his father was a boy.

"Didn't know you could read, Em," one of the men had quipped.

Emerson was too excited to rise to the bait. "Frank Merriwell could pitch a double shoot."

"Did you just make that up, Em?"

"The ball would start to curve out and then at the last minute it would curve back in towards the batter."

"You don't say! You'll have to teach Denehy how to do that."

Denehy was an explosive pitcher, and on this cold day in

Murmansk he worked through his routine of warm-up stretches while Steve, already helmeted, stamped around on the snow taking practice swings with his bat. Keith located centre field. This was usually Emerson's position, but he was umpire today, having sprained his ankle the previous evening.

Emerson took his duties as umpire so seriously that the men left off ribbing him for the most part, although Steve acted the clown at times. He would assume a ferocious expression, pumping his arms and legs, as he raced past third base before sliding into home. Or he would run in an exaggeratedly slow manner, prompting cries from Denehy.

"He's like an old lady with wet drawers, ain't he, fellas?"

Throughout the game, the oldest of the three Russian youngsters chased after balls, returning them to the pitcher; that is, all except the last ball. The kid must have had a sixth sense: the men had just decided to call it a day when Steve exclaimed, "The little rascal! He's run off with our ball."

The two younger boys and the sledge had also disappeared.

"He'll sell it to the next lot of unsuspecting Americans," Keith laughed.

Keith wrote a second letter to Jeanne while in Murmansk:

My dearest Jeanne,

To my great joy, I received three letters from you last week. I sorted them carefully into date order, just as I used to do when I was stationed in a certain very hot place that I grew to know only too well.

At your training school they work you hard, but it seems to me, reading between the lines, that you are blossoming. That makes me happy. One day, when you are a qualified nurse, you will be able to travel anywhere in the world. You would like America, even though it is far from Scotland and a thousand times bigger. People are friendly and there is work there for both of us, not just in the big cities but in country areas too.

We had a bit of excitement recently (if that is the correct word) when some of the merchant crew—we didn't find out who—smuggled two girls on board and stowed them in one of the holds. I was the one who discovered them, and I had no option but to report it to the captain. Then I had to put on my fierce Armed Guard hat and, together with one of the other men, Cormac Denehy, our biggest, burliest fellow, guard the girls in the captain's quarters until the authorities arrived to remove them from the ship. Once word about the incident got around, some of the older hands muttered that it was bad luck for the ship to have women aboard.

Young Emerson, whom I think I've mentioned to you before, has of course managed to get himself into trouble. The authorities came aboard to escort him away on some minor charge, and the ship's captain, who I'm sure privately considers Emerson an idiot, practically exploded. "You cannot take anybody off my ship. This is my ship, and under the American flag!" The captain won the day, and the authorities beat a speedy retreat.

To turn to happier topics, we had a party on board the other night. The excuse was the chief engineer's birthday. He's very popular, like a father figure to the younger men. Even our unpredictable chief cook likes him, and he baked a huge yeast cake with a thick, creamy filling. One of the merchant boys who performed with a big band in New York before the war played his trumpet. The sound drifted through the still night air, and men on both sides of the ship came out on deck to listen, and we all got emotional and began thinking of home, family and sweethearts.

Well, my sweetheart, on that note I'll end.

I am well, and I send all my love.

Beidh grá agam duit dtólamh.

Keith

During the six weeks the *Harold Beacon* was tied up in Murmansk, when boredom replaced exhaustion, Keith no longer fell asleep as soon as his head hit his pillow at night. Lying there listening to the snores and grunts and farts of his buddies, he would transport himself to Montana. It would be five or six years in the future, and the war would be well over. He would be tanned and healthy and relaxed, out in the open all day, working on a huge sheep ranch. The rancher would be a kindly silver-haired man with a Scottish brogue like his own, and they would ride the prairies together. He would not be lonely because Jeanne would be in Montana too, legally, as a trained nurse. And when their work for the day was done, he and Jeanne would sit together on the veranda and discuss their plans for the future.

It was more than a dream; it was something to hold on to. That's what Vi Spaulding had said the last time she wrote. She told him she had an address for him, passed on by a young New Zealand airman whose uncle had gone to Montana from Scotland before the First World War.

Preparations were made for the convoy to leave Murmansk and there were arguments with the Russians over the ballast necessary to ensure stability of the ships, now they had been emptied of their cargoes. The first mate of the *Harold Beacon* estimated they had been given at most 1,600 tons of ballast, not the minimum 2,000 tons requested. He also said there were chunks of frozen sand mixed in with the fine sand and gravel.

The masters of the merchant ships were notified that they would have passengers on the return voyage. News had been received of German attacks on Norwegian patriots on the island of Sørøya, and four destroyers from the convoy's escort had been ordered to the scene to rescue them. Five hundred men, women and children were to be distributed among the ships of the convoy for passage to England.

During the afternoon and evening of February 16, the destroyers moved from merchantman to merchantman, transferring small parties of Norwegians across. The crew of the *Harold Beacon* watched, curious, as nineteen refugees were conveyed to her decks, and the ship's purser took charge of them. The Norwegians were mostly women and children, but there were three men, fathers of families, in the group. They were very quiet, in ragged clothes, and all looked exhausted. Word was they had been living in caves on Sørøya. The *Harold Beacon* was not equipped to accommodate extra passengers, and some of the crew members had to double up to house the refugees.

The crew were informed that they would depart Murmansk the following day. The convoy would be made up of thirty-five merchant ships, and it would have a heavy escort: a cruiser, two escort carriers, six corvettes and ten destroyers. No one expressed sorrow at leaving Murmansk. Despite the dangers ahead, they all wanted to be on their way.

Chapter 27

On departure day, word came that a Nazi wolf pack lay in wait off the entrance to Kola Bay. The escorts had cleared the approaches the evening before and went out again and swept the area. The merchant ships were ordered to follow two abreast at top speed and to form up in a convoy later. This was done messily, and the *Harold Beacon*, hitherto well forward in the convoy, ended up in one of the vulnerable outermost positions at the rear—the "coffin corner".

The convoy was steaming in an easterly direction before turning to the north-west at the end of the swept channel leading out from Murmansk when Keith, who was out on deck, noticed the corvette HMS *Bluebell* nearby. This small warship, in her blue-and-white camouflage paint and measuring less than half the length of the *Harold Beacon*, was busily making her way round the edge of the convoy. He was watching the men working on her deck when there was a blinding flash and a roar and a violent shock wave rocked the *Harold Beacon*, knocking him off balance.

We've been hit.

The thought rushed into Keith's mind, followed immediately by the realisation that this was not so. He watched in horror as a tower of smoke and dull red flame enveloped the *Bluebell* and rose a thousand feet into the air. When the smoke cleared, there remained no trace of the *Bluebell*, just an oily slick on the water and a scattering of lifeless bodies. There was a momentary deathly silence, and then the alarms began shrieking. The men rushed to their action stations, where they talked to each other in hushed voices as the escorts dropped depth charges and the convoy steamed on.

That evening after dinner, Keith sat in the mess with a solemn-faced group of men. Ollie Daisley, one of the oilers from the engine room, a thin, highly strung individual, began to shuffle a pack of cards. His hands shook. "Anyone want a game of poker? Gin rummy? Euchre?"

The others shook their heads.

"Poor buggers," Ollie said. "They didn't stand a chance."

Word was that the destroyer detailed to pick up survivors from the *Bluebell* found only three. The crew of the *Harold Beacon* did not know what state these three men were in, or even if they were still alive.

"The chief told us," Ollie continued, "that Captain Caruso promised him, if our ship gets hit by a torpedo Captain will let him know immediately so we're not trapped down below."

Keith nodded. He knew, because they had talked about it before, that the greatest fear of those who worked beneath the waterline was being trapped below, imprisoned down there with the water rushing in.

The threat of U-boats subsided and there were a few days of uneasy calm. One morning Keith was on duty beside his gun when he suddenly realised someone was speaking to him.

"I know how to use guns. I can help you."

Keith gave a start. He had been almost asleep on his feet. He had not noticed the Norwegian man, who had walked up quietly behind him and now addressed him in halting but clear English. "Thank you," Keith said, "but I wouldn't be allowed to accept."

The man was about fifty, lean and fit looking with a deeply lined face. He nodded slowly and then extended his hand. "My name is Pedersen. I was also at sea, when a young man. I learned to speak some English. Only one on Sørøya to speak English."

"Stay and talk to me," Keith said. "The watches are long when you haven't had any sleep."

"I know about watching. On Sørøya I always watched. For the Germans, in case they came back."

"The Germans made life hard for you."

"They take our young men and women, to work. They kill

our animals. They burn our food crops."

"You must have been very hungry."

"I hunt for reindeer. I catch fish. So the women and children do not starve."

"They said you had to live in caves."

"Yes. In caves and in the snow. After the Germans burn our houses. Now we have to leave Sørøya forever."

"It is hard when you know you cannot go home again."

"Yes. But we are thankful that your ships come, to rescue our women and children."

Keith talked to him about the work he did, and the guns his team used, until Pedersen took his leave, saying, "I will come and talk to you again."

The following day, as the convoy passed through a narrow strip of sea between the north coast of Norway and the Arctic ice, near Bear Island, a new enemy arrived, an enemy far more powerful than U-boats.

Chapter 28

Norwegian Sea
February 1945

Keith gripped the sides of the gun box as the spray swept over his head and froze on his clothes. He wore a bulky life jacket on top of a heavy oilskin coat, with multiple warm layers underneath, heavy leather sea boots, with two pairs of knitted sea boot stockings, but he was freezing cold. For two days now, since the night of February 17, a violent storm had raged. He had been told the winds were gusting to sixty knots and had reached force 10 on the Beaufort scale. The gun box dipped and rose as the port side of the *Harold Beacon* dipped and rose on monstrous seas higher than houses. There was no real shelter for him. It was two o'clock in the morning, two hours into the middle watch, but in this howling darkness he could see nothing, not even a single distress light. The escorts and the other ships must have been out there somewhere, but perhaps they were scattered far away.

Two hours later, relieved by one of the other gunners, Keith stumbled down to the mess and sank on to a seat at one of the tables. The table was firmly bolted to the floor, but everything else—plates, knives, forks—rattled and slid as the ship rolled. To his surprise, Krakowski was in the mess, seated with his large belly firmly wedged against a table.

He looked Keith up and down, and then hauled himself awkwardly to his feet, saying, "Wait here." He disappeared for a short time, returning with a cup of coffee and a large sandwich stuffed with corned beef.

Keith gratefully devoured the sandwich and the hot drink, then went to his quarters and fell asleep immediately.

By the following morning, the storm had eased somewhat, although conditions were still rough. Two escort ships arrived and shepherded the *Harold Beacon* back into her position in the rear of the convoy. All the other ships had already been rounded up. Then, at around ten a.m., the alarms began jangling once again. The men ran wearily to their battle stations to confront another attack. This time, two dozen German torpedo bombers struck at the convoy. Despite the heaving seas, several Wildcat fighter planes managed to get off the flight deck of the convoy's baby flattop HMS *Nairana* to engage the enemy.

The battle raged for three hours, with the escorting warships and the Armed Guards on the merchant ships raking the skies until, at last, the aggressors retired. No ships had been lost from the convoy, nor any of the fighter planes.

Now, however, the men were at their battle stations continuously as they waited for the next attack. The gunners took turns sleeping out in the weather in their gun tubs. It became obvious that the *Harold Beacon* was falling behind the rest of the convoy. News was that the storm had damaged her steering mechanism and Chief Franklin and his team were working around the clock to try to fix it.

On the night of February 22, off Norway's Lofoten Islands, a second storm struck. But this storm was force 12 on the Beaufort scale. A hurricane. Terrifying winds buffeted the *Harold Beacon*, and waves fifty to sixty feet high lashed the main deck, the boat deck and even the flying bridge. No one except the gunner on watch was allowed to go out on deck.

Keith clung to the railing and eyed the ladder he needed to climb. He let go and was sent sprawling. So he crawled. He reached the ladder and began hauling himself up. The wind screamed; and the rain, laden with ice, stung his face. The lurching of the ship meant that his body rotated through an arc, one side then the other. He imagined he felt the inadequate ballast shifting in the ship's bowels. At what point would she capsize? Forty degrees? Fifty degrees? Sixty degrees?

As he reached the top of the ladder, clinging to the handrails, he sensed that the *Harold Beacon* had altered her course, or perhaps the waves had changed direction. They were like skyscrapers the colour of steel but lacking windows or light.

The *Harold Beacon* groaned and laboured as she fought her way from the depth of a trough and Keith fought his way to the gun tub. Aidan O'Connell, whom he was replacing on watch, was crouched against the tub. He looked up, relief on his face, when Keith called out. Soon he would be in the mess warming body and soul with coffee and food.

Why are we out here in the elements watching? Keith asked himself. *Bombers can't fly in a hurricane. They'll be confined to their bases. The enemy now is the wind, and the sea.*

But he knew the answer to his question. And he knew that Captain Caruso would be maintaining his post on the bridge, directing the ship day and night without sleeping, until the hurricane died.

After he came off duty, Keith went into the mess, where many of the men had congregated, as there was little chance of getting any sleep. The *Harold Beacon*'s engines had slowed to an idle and she had developed a heavy list. Keith noticed that instead of looking into the eyes of those seated on the opposite side of the table, he looked above their heads. The men already wore their kapok life jackets day and night, but now some of the merchant crew had also donned the Arctic rubber suits they had been issued. All but two of the *Harold Beacon*'s lifeboats had been carried away or damaged, and the life rafts had been torn from their lashings.

Steve and the other signalman remained with Captain Caruso on the bridge all night long. At midnight, the blue stern lights of some of the other vessels in the convoy were still visible bobbing in the distance, but by three thirty the next morning they had disappeared from sight again. At around this time the *Harold Beacon*'s engines stopped and she started to drift.

By five o'clock in the morning the storm was subsiding. The engine room team had got the *Harold Beacon*'s engines started again and she began to make reasonably good speed. The other ships were nowhere in sight, but Captain Caruso had returned his ship to the course set for the convoy many hours before and he kept a lookout posted in the crow's nest. Wartime regulations forbade the *Harold Beacon* from transmitting messages, but there was a Marconi receiver in the pilot house on the bridge, which meant the officer on watch could receive messages. At approximately ten thirty a.m., a warning came through from the convoy flagship: all ships were alerted for an attack by German aircraft.

Captain Caruso sounded the general alarm, the gunners and crewmen rushed to their battle stations and the ship braced for attack. As he waited at his gun with Lincoln, Keith thought to himself that they were alone in this vast ocean; the rest of the convoy was perhaps fifty miles away, not even aware the *Harold Beacon* was missing, and there was no one to protect them but themselves and God, for those who believed. He looked across at the other starboard Oerlikon and saw Aidan, a devout Catholic, with his lips moving in prayer and his fingers tracing his rosary beads.

The minutes passed. An hour, then several hours went by, and there was still no sign of the Luftwaffe. Tensions began to ease. The merchant seamen assisting at the guns drifted off in twos and threes for chow. Keith and the other gunners sat at their guns and were served sandwiches and coffee in buckets.

Suddenly, at about one thirty in the afternoon, Keith felt the *Harold Beacon* slow down. Then she made a turn, a full 180 degrees. There was an outbreak of nervous babble from the gunners. Soon afterwards, Steve Allison came and told them that Captain Caruso had decided to reverse direction and retrace the *Harold Beacon*'s course, on the chance that she had overtaken the rest of the convoy when it stopped to regroup following the hurricane. Steve said they could still hear the convoy escorts on the radiotelephone, and Caruso was convinced he was closing in on the convoy. He had even offered a five-dollar bill to the first man who sighted it.

About half an hour later, something materialised on the horizon off the starboard bow.

"Maybe it's the convoy catching us up," one of the gunners said.

"Nah. More like a line of geese flying low."

"Ducks, perhaps."

The men continued to peer at the horizon, as the tiny forms became larger.

Keith watched through his binoculars. "It's not ducks. It's a squadron of planes."

"Maybe they're fighters from our flattop," Lincoln suggested.

Keith was counting. "There are twenty-three of them." As the planes came closer he said, "They're not fighters. They're twin-engine bombers. German." He counted them twice more. "It's a squadron of Ju 88s."

One of the others said, "Surely they won't bother with one old Liberty ship. They must know there's a whole convoy somewhere nearby."

But the planes were flying low. They had a target in sight. And the *Harold Beacon*'s alarm was sounding. A life-or-death battle was about to begin: one weary, limping merchant ship against twenty-three Junkers torpedo bombers.

Chapter 29

Here they come!" a voice shouted, as the bomber squadron bore down on the *Harold Beacon*. Sleek, dark planes bearing swastikas and two torpedoes slung on racks beneath their bellies approached in wing-to-wing formation in groups of three.

Lieutenant Savela acted with icy calm. "Hold your fire," he commanded, "until the planes are closer."

The seconds ticked by in an eternity. At last, when the planes were perhaps a thousand yards away, Savela shouted, "Fire!"

Every gun on the *Harold Beacon* fired simultaneously, drowning out the roar of the Ju 88s.

The first plane peeled off for the attack. It dropped its torpedo at the stern of the *Harold Beacon* and made off unscarred. Then the second plane bore down so close that Keith could see the pilot's face. Suddenly the plane exploded in mid-air as a shell from the five-inch gun manned by Cormac Denehy and his crew tore into the plane's nose. Flaming debris spun into the ocean, sending up a geyser of water as it disappeared. None of the four-man crew surfaced.

Captain Caruso, pacing up and down in the wheelhouse, shouted, "Well done, my boys!"

Keith could not help but feel amused that Caruso should suddenly be calling the naval gunners "my boys".

The bombers scattered beyond the range of the *Harold Beacon*'s guns and began to circle the ship in a deadly dance. They made another run at the *Harold Beacon*, but her luck held. The twenty- to thirty-foot waves and the moving target meant not one of the torpedoes found its mark.

On the upper bridge, the chief mate and the second mate were observing the quick succession of torpedoes discharged by the attacking planes. The chief mate shouted down orders to the wheelhouse:

"Hard to starboard!"

"Hard to port!"

"As you were!"

The *Harold Beacon* began to zigzag evasively, tugging heavily on her damaged steering apparatus. The torpedoes bounced and turned when they hit the rough water. Some dived straight down beneath the surface; others skipped from wave to wave, exploding harmlessly in the sea near the ship.

The Germans made run after run. All around was the cacophony of the struggle: the thunder of aircraft engines, the fierce crackle of machine-gun fire, the intermittent blast of the *Harold Beacon*'s two big guns and the thin shriek of falling shrapnel.

The gunners hit a second plane and then a third. Both planes spiralled downwards, belching smoke and bright tongues of flame, and sank into the sea. The men on deck stared with morbid fascination as one torpedo after another streaked past the ship in a flash of white and disappeared into the deep. A fourth plane fell, struck by the crossfire of the two port Oerlikons.

Keith's crew of machine gunners poured out hundreds of rounds of 20 mm shells, fifty-eight rounds every eight or nine seconds. His Oerlikon heated up to the point where a shell lodged in the breech. He slipped out of his harness and forced the shell partway out by recocking the gun, then Lincoln grabbed the hot shell with his bare hands and threw it overboard. Keith quickly reharnessed himself, and Lincoln slammed home a magazine just in time for Keith to lower his gun and explode a torpedo skipping through the water towards the ship. The explosion threw up a geyser that sprayed the deck. Lincoln let out a little cheer, but Keith knew it was only a matter of time: how could one Liberty ship, on its own, hold off a squadron of bombers?

Word came around that the *Harold Beacon*'s radio officers had sent out messages and had received a signal from a land station in Scotland. There was, however, still no news that the convoy escorts knew where they were or had even received the *Harold Beacon*'s communications.

More than three dozen torpedoes had been dropped. The *Harold Beacon* was still unscathed, but at least four German planes had been shot down. Two others were damaged—they billowed smoke—and the remaining planes now circled out of range of the *Harold Beacon*'s guns. The rough seas, the evasive action directed from the bridge and the firepower from the gun tubs had combined to spoil the aim of the enemy.

"Maybe the Germans have used up all their torpedoes. Maybe they're giving up," Lincoln said.

"Don't count on it," Keith said. But he allowed himself a flickering hope that Lincoln might be correct. Perhaps the skilled seamanship of Captain Caruso and his crew, and their own expertise as gunners, had allowed them to defy fate.

He got his answer a few minutes later. Away on the port side, one of the planes broke away from the other Ju 88s and tilted into a long dive towards the stern of the *Harold Beacon*. The plane banked and then dropped its two torpedoes. There was a call of "Hard to starboard" from the wing of the bridge, but this time the ship did not zigzag away from the torpedoes hurling towards her. Perhaps her damaged steering apparatus had finally given up.

The crew of the Ju 88 paid the full price for their actions. Their plane was caught by gunfire from the *Harold Beacon* and went down under a rain of shells, sinking instantly. At almost the same moment, a deafening detonation rocked the ship. Hatch covers and debris went flying into the air, and the main mast came crashing down. The force of the explosion threw one of the men from the port Oerlikons over his gun and on to the fantail. His battle helmet protected his head, but he was shaken, and it was a moment before he could crawl back.

The remaining Ju 88s still circled out there.

Where did the torpedo hit us? Keith asked himself. *It must be one of the holds on the port side. The* Beacon *heeled over to starboard before she righted herself.*

The *Harold Beacon* began to settle in the stern. Two of the gunners stationed in that part of the ship came and told Savela that the ship appeared to be sinking.

"Stand by your guns!" Savela replied sharply, and the men returned to their posts.

As the ship settled, Captain Caruso signalled to the German planes that the *Harold Beacon* was "target destroyed." Slowly, the remaining bombers regrouped and began to head back to their base, leaving one plane to circle at a distance.

Captain Caruso sent two of his officers to make a personal inspection and evaluate the damage. They reported that the ship's side had split from number five hold, where the torpedo had struck, to midship, and she was taking in water fast. The deck was ripped open, with huge gaps visible. Bulkheads and steam lines had ruptured. The crew were trying to seal off flooded areas.

Caruso promptly informed the men down in the engine room, and a few minutes later the *Harold Beacon*'s engine came to a halt for the final time. Shortly afterwards, the engine room crew, led by Chief Franklin, climbed up the ladder on to the deck. Among them was Ollie Daisley, his face pale and haunted.

Pedersen had run out on deck immediately after the torpedo hit and helped care for those who had received minor injuries. Now the other Norwegian refugees gathered on the boat deck and waited silently and stoically, ready to obey orders.

On the bridge, Captain Caruso calmly gave orders and received reports of damage. He asked the chief radio officer to send an SOS and the *Harold Beacon*'s position. Again, a land station in Scotland acknowledged the message. This time there was also a faint single-digit response from the convoy.

Then Captain Caruso gave the order to abandon ship.

Chapter 30

Lieutenant Savela signalled the men down from their gun posts, and Keith made his way to the boat deck with the others. The last to arrive were Denehy and his crew from the five-inch gun.

"Had to wade through knee-deep water," Denehy said, "and climb over wood and other shit scattered around the gun tub. The area's torn up real bad."

On the boat deck, Captain Caruso, with the bosun at his side, was issuing commands. He ordered the Norwegian refugees into the first of the two usable lifeboats, along with five crew members to help them handle it. Then he turned to the chief radio officer and asked, "You have sent all the distress signals?"

"Yes, sir."

"You have dumped all secret and confidential documents?"

"Yes, sir."

"Then you are assigned to this lifeboat too, so you can install and handle the emergency radio equipment. If our ship goes down," he added, "that little transmitter will be our only way to communicate with the rescue ships."

Some of the Armed Guard were responsible for the large rafts. One raft had been damaged by the explosion, but the men managed to get the other three into the water, and they remained attached to the ship. However, before the rafts could be used, someone panicked and released all the ropes. The strong wind and ten-foot waves soon carried the rafts far away.

⁓◦∞◦⁓

Keith climbed forward to the bow, where he had noticed Ollie trying to free the small, two-man raft that was lashed to the three-inch gun. Ollie's movements were rushed, almost frenzied.

"Hold on, I'll give you a hand!" Keith called out.

Ollie raised his head. His eyes stared blankly ahead, and his mouth was working. Then, he picked up a fire axe and began swinging it at Keith.

Keith ducked out of range and shouted, "Ollie! Stop! Let me help you."

Ollie appeared to hear nothing. Wildly brandishing the axe, he turned to the cork raft and proceeded to chop it into pieces. Then he dropped the axe to the ground, rushed to the side of the ship and threw himself into the sea.

Keith stood rooted to the spot. At last he turned and made his way back to the boat deck.

The bosun was examining one of the heavy beams that had been used to cradle the locomotives they carried to Murmansk. "That lumber could make a raft."

"Then let's do it," Keith said.

The two men, assisted by others, made two rafts by forming a rectangle with four beams and lashing the ends together with rope. On top of this they tied heavy planks from the hatches and deck. After completing the rafts they turned them over to others to use.

"And it's payday too," muttered one of the deckhands as he and five others took possession of a raft.

Keith understood what he meant. If a merchant seaman's ship was sunk, his pay stopped that day.

Keith went to his quarters. It was freezing cold; all the warmth had left the ship. He checked his clothing and then picked up the fine woollen scarf he had bought for Jeanne and tucked it round his neck, against his skin.

He found Steve in the signalmen's quarters examining a rubber life-saving suit.

"One of the merchant boys gave me this," Steve said. "I'm debating whether to wear it or not."

"Don't even think of it," Keith warned. "If we end up in the water and you're wearing one of those, you'll sink like a rock."

Steve did not argue. They had been ordered not to accept these rubber suits if offered to them. They were cumbersome, easily punctured and often cracked, split or leaked in the closures or around the neckband. Such a suit would quickly fill with water and drag the wearer under.

Steve laid his hand on his beautiful big Bible. Keith wondered if he planned to take it with him, but he wrapped it in a scarf and put it down again. Then he took the photo of his wife from its frame, folded it, and placed it in his inside pocket.

Keith and Steve climbed to the boat deck where the second lifeboat was about to be launched. Men were gathered there, reticent to step forward. Captain Caruso insisted that the naval gunners get their share of seats, and Keith and Lieutenant Savela were among those assigned to the boat.

"I'd like some volunteers to stay on the machine guns on the bridge in case the Germans return," Savela called out.

"I'll stay, sir," Keith said without hesitation.

"I'll go with you," volunteered Denehy.

"And I'll go too," said Steve.

Savela gave his quiet, warm smile. "Thanks, boys. And good luck."

The three volunteers remained on deck as the gunners climbed into the lifeboat, followed by members of the crew, including Chief Engineer Franklin.

"You should have gone with them," Keith said to Steve. "You've got a wife."

"And you've got a sweetheart." He gave Keith a playful punch. "Anyway, someone has to keep you in check."

"It's only right I should stay," Keith said. "I'm the one responsible for the Oerlikons." He looked at Denehy. "But what about you, Cormac?"

"I've been in cold water before. I've always been able to shift for myself."

The boat was about to be lowered into the sea when Chief Franklin looked up at young Hopkins, who was still on the deck. He called to him, "Get into the boat, kid. Take my place. I've lived my life. It doesn't matter so much if I don't return." With that he climbed out of the lifeboat and back on to the deck of the sinking ship.

Pushed by others, the boy took his seat. There were twenty-seven men in a boat with capacity for twenty.

Keith watched as the groaning lifeboat was lowered into the water. He felt curiously detached, as though in a dream.

As Keith walked away with the other two, Steve indicated a bulky figure crouched awkwardly on the deck. It was Jake Krakowski, rendering first aid to a man who had been wounded by flying debris.

Krakowski raised his head and Keith caught his eye. The two nodded gravely at each other before Krakowski returned to his task.

"I never got the measure of that man," Steve said. "So prickly and unpleasant. And yet—"

"With the ability to surprise, right to the end."

The three men returned to the bridge. Keith put a full magazine into the forward gun portside, and Denehy did the same on the aft gun. The lone German plane observing them was too far away to hit, but Keith decided to let the crew know the *Harold Beacon*'s guns were still operating. He fired one last burst, and the plane flew further away until it disappeared.

A new plane appeared on the horizon, this time from the starboard side. Keith climbed back into the gun tub and strapped himself in. As the plane came gradually closer, he moved the gun barrel around and watched the plane in the spiderweb of the sight. He lay back in the harness of his Oerlikon, moving the barrel smoothly, waiting for the exact moment when the plane would be close enough but not too close. Then suddenly he relaxed. This was not another German bomber: it was a Grumman Wildcat, one of the planes from the convoy's flattop. What courage and airmanship to take off in these conditions.

He unstrapped himself and went to the bridge house in time to hear Captain Caruso ask Steve to send an SOS. The plane blinked in reply that help was on its way, and Steve repeated the message out loud to the men nearby. They let out a cheer. Then the plane dipped its wings and flew away.

"Now we know for certain they are coming to help us," Captain Caruso said. "They have three hours at most before it is completely dark."

When the water reached the deck of the bridge, Keith knew it was time to leave. He went with Steve and Denehy to farewell Captain Caruso. Steve carried an extra life jacket and he tried to persuade Caruso to put it on, but the captain simply let it slide to the floor. Chief Franklin, who stood beside him wearing a life jacket over his sheepskin coat, gave a small smile and shook his head.

Captain Caruso and Chief Franklin wished Keith and the other two good luck, and they shook hands as they separated. Then the three navy men turned to go, while the captain and the chief walked slowly back to the bridge house.

The *Harold Beacon* was now poised at a 45-degree angle. If they were going to leave, it was now or never. The three men removed their Arctic boots and helmets and checked their life jackets.

Steve put his hands on the shoulders of the other two as he prayed aloud, "Dear God, take us into your care and protection and give us strength. Watch over our ship and the men still aboard her as well as those in the water. And care for our loved ones at home while we are separated from them. We ask this in your name. Amen."

They walked to the aft end of the bridge and stepped over the side, into the Arctic Ocean.

Keith broke the surface gasping, fighting to drag air into his lungs. Steve and Denehy had surfaced too. He could hear their cries. The three men began swimming, desperate to get away from the *Harold Beacon* before she sank and pulled them down with her. Their heavy clothing was soon saturated, and their movements grew slower and slower.

They had managed perhaps thirty yards when the dying ship

reared up, towering above them. Suddenly she was rocked by an explosion, and there was a loud hissing sound as the air rushed from her bowels. A hail of debris shot from the decks, landing in the water around them, and a heavy ventilator that had been forced free crashed down on Steve and Denehy.

"My arm," Steve cried out.

There was no sound from Denehy.

Keith swam to his side and found him with his skull burst and his eyes vacant. Cormac Denehy, the man with the heart of an ox, gone in an instant.

He looked closely at Denehy's face, gently touched his forehead and whispered, *"Gus am bris an là, a'bràthair."* Then he turned away, calling out, "Denehy's dead. There's nothing we can do for him. We have to get ourselves out of the water or we'll be dead too."

"My arm's broken," Steve said. "I can't use it."

Keith spotted the roof of the wheelhouse, which had blown off in the explosion, and motioned Steve to swim towards it. He climbed on to the roof, then helped Steve, whose right arm was hanging uselessly.

Just as the two of them crawled out of the sea, the mortally wounded ship gave a deep sigh and slid quietly down beneath the water. SS *Harold Beacon*. Born on November 11, 1942, in Wilmington, North Carolina. Died February 23, 1945, in the Norwegian Sea. Until four hours earlier, home to forty-eight merchant seamen and officers, twenty-seven Naval Armed Guard plus their commander, and eighteen Norwegian refugees. Now the tomb and last resting place of Captain Alfred Caruso, Chief Engineer Don Franklin and a handful of others still on board when she sank.

Keith and Steve squatted on their knees, shaking with the brutal cold. They took it in turns to stumble to their feet and rub their legs to keep the blood circulating. Shortly afterwards, Lincoln and one of the deckhands floated into sight on a two-man raft. The two were singing "I've Got a Lovely Bunch of Coconuts."

"Follow us, boys," Keith joked. "It's this way."

Lincoln gave a mock salute and started a round of "Roll out the Barrel."

Keith and Steve joined in, but were left singing on their own as the action of the water took the other two out of view again.

The ocean was lonely and empty without their ship. All that remained now was the cold wind whistling around them, a little snow, and scattered pieces of debris bearing frightened and freezing men who cried out occasionally. Also somewhere nearby but out of sight drifted two lifeboats and some rafts.

Once, as the wheelhouse roof hovered on the crest of wave, Keith spotted Lieutenant Savela and some gunners on a navy raft. They must have found one of the rafts that drifted away from the *Harold Beacon* and transferred across from the overcrowded lifeboat.

Keith and Steve had been in the sea for at least fifteen minutes when a whistle sounded nearby. Someone clinging to a piece of timber blew frantically on the whistle attached to his life jacket. There was a faint cry: "Help."

"It's Emerson," Steve shouted. "Swim over to us."

Emerson relinquished his grip on the timber and began swimming towards Keith and Steve. They called out, "You can make it, buddy."

At last Emerson reached the makeshift raft, and Keith dragged him aboard. Emerson's hands were freezing cold, his teeth chattered and he shivered violently. Keith rubbed Emerson's body, trying to restore the circulation. He and Steve continued taking turns to force themselves to their feet, but Emerson was too weak to do so. Eventually Keith and Steve stopped too.

They pressed close to each other, Emerson directly in front of Keith, and Steve at Keith's side.

Steve prayed out loud, "Dear God, please help us, as you have helped us before. We pray that we may be found before darkness falls."

A flock of seagulls flew over.

"Look, Emerson. It's a signal there's someone nearby," Keith said. Privately he wondered if it meant they were drifting near the Norwegian coast with its German bases.

Emerson had stopped shivering. "Say a prayer for me," he said to Keith. "No one ever taught me how to pray."

"I can't pray the way Steve does," Keith said. "I'll say the Twenty-third Psalm for you. I learned Bible verses at Sunday school. The Lord is my shepherd; I shall not want."

Emerson had become very still.

"Say it with me, Emerson."

He heard Emerson murmur something.

"He maketh me to lie down in green pastures: he leadeth me beside the still waters." He paused as a rough wave lifted the wheelhouse.

"Don't stop," Emerson said in a weak voice.

"He restoreth my soul: he leadeth me in the paths of righteousness for his name's sake."

Emerson was very quiet, his breathing gentle, barely audible.

"Yea, though I walk through the valley of the shadow of death, I will fear no evil: for thou art with me; thy rod and thy staff they comfort me. Thou preparest a table before me in the presence of mine enemies: thou annointest my head with oil; my cup runneth over."

Emerson's head rested against him.

"Surely goodness and mercy shall follow me all the days of my life: and I will dwell in the house of the Lord for ever."

He had reached the end, and so he simply crouched there with his arm over Emerson's shoulder, supporting him. He became aware that Steve was speaking to him.

"Keith. Let him go."

He continued to cradle Emerson with his arm.

"Keith. He's foaming at the mouth. Emerson is dead. You can't do anything for him now. Let him go."

Keith squeezed Emerson against him until finally releasing his grip. Emerson remained upright for a while. Then, as they were lifted roughly on another wave, he slowly toppled to one side and fell into the Arctic Ocean and disappeared from sight. Keith kept his eyes fixed on the spot where Emerson had been, while Steve said a prayer committing his body to the deep. Emerson, their immature young friend, who should have had time to grow into manhood and live a long life.

"When all this is over we'll visit Emerson's parents," Steve said. "We'll tell them their son didn't die alone. He died a peaceful death in the arms of a friend."

Keith and Steve huddled together and forced each other to keep talking. They talked about serious things, and silly things like nicknames they had heard: "Dinger" for Bell, "Nosy" for Parker, "Sheep's Arse" for Winterbottom. When they ran short of topics, they thought up names for Lieutenant Savela's unborn child.

Keith's feet were like blocks of ice but his body felt oddly warm. He saw something red in the sky and thought he was hallucinating.

"Steve, can you see a light up there?" he asked.

Steve did not answer straight away. Then he said, "It's a flare. Look, there's another one. The men in the lifeboats are firing the Very pistols. They've spotted a ship."

The two of them let out a weak cheer and waited. There was not much time. Darkness fell early in these latitudes.

Keith tried to focus his eyes. Was that smudge in the distance a destroyer? The wheelhouse roof went down into a trough and the grey shape disappeared, but then they were lifted again on the peak of a wave, and he saw he was not mistaken. The ship gradually moved closer, or perhaps they were the ones who moved closer, carried by the waves. He had lost all sense of time. Only one thing was important: to keep holding on.

He saw figures leaning over from the deck of the destroyer, and also a net and lines hanging down. Right alongside the destroyer, a battered raft bobbed with men on it, and he realised it was Lieutenant Savela and a small crew. The figures on the deck hauled the men up one by one. A big wave almost tossed him and Steve off their perch and he put his head down and gripped hard, Next time he saw the ship, the raft was still there but all the men were gone. The destroyer began moving slowly towards them.

"Hold on, Keith," said Steve.

Suddenly the destroyer was right beside them. Men leaned over the rails and threw down a rope with a grappling hook on the end.

Keith called in his loudest voice, gesturing at Steve, "His arm is broken."

A man on deck called out in return and demonstrated with his hands. "Attach the hook to his life vest!"

Keith's frozen hands were thick and clumsy as he grabbed the hook. He had trouble moving his fingers. After a struggle, he managed to attach the hook to Steve's vest.

"Thanks, Buddy," Steve said.

The men on the deck began hauling Steve up. *Not long now*, Keith said to himself.

Steve was halfway up the side of the ship when it happened. In slow motion, his body began to peel away from the hook. One of the men on the deck shouted, but there was no sound from Steve. Then Steve dropped down into the sea. Keith tried to jump in after him, but he was unable to move.

He gazed up at the destroyer. High above him a flag fluttered, but it was not the battered Stars and Stripes from the *Harold Beacon*. It was a white flag with the Union Jack in one corner. A fog closed in and voices called faintly. Perhaps one of them was Jeanne, come to meet him? He breathed her name.

But no, it was not Jeanne. It was his mother. And his brother was beside her. It had been so long. Keith's body filled with warmth.

And now there was a man, tall and bearded, with chiselled features.

He searched the man's face, expecting to see disapproval.

Instead, he saw that the man's eyes were kind and welcoming.

And the man was reaching out his hand to him. Reaching out his hand.

Chapter 31

Glasgow
February 1945

Two young women, wearing heavy scarlet capes over white uniforms, stepped out from the entrance to the Glasgow Royal Infirmary and paused at the top of the steps. Behind them was the Templeton Building, eight floors of solid, symmetrical stone, relieved only by round turrets at the corners. Ahead of them, beyond the yard and the gate, was Castle Street.

The taller of the two women took a deep breath. "Ah, fresh air. And freedom."

"Aye, it's fresh arricht, if you mean cold," her companion said, "but I dinna ken how clean it is."

"Anything's fresh after the sluice room. Do you know how many bedpans I washed this morning, Sheila?"

"Three hundred?"

"Sixty."

"Jeanne MacKenzie, have you forgotten the very recent words of Miss McIntosh, your favourite sister tutor?" Sheila stuck out her neck like a turkey, bobbing her head back and forth. "Gurrls, you will soon be probationer nurses, and you must never forget, it is the wee things that are important. A bedpan which does not shine like a mirror casts a bad light on the honourable profession of nursing."

Jeanne laughed. "Come on. She didn't say that. Well, not exactly. It's just that I didn't expect so many."

They hastened down the steps and had almost reached the

gate when an elderly gentleman heading in the same direction doffed his hat and stood aside, saying, "After you, nurse."

"There you are," Sheila whispered to Jeanne. "At least someone thinks you're a real nurse."

Sheila and Jeannie turned left at the gate and, arms linked, walked the short distance to St Mungo's Cathedral, a building of late medieval design, dwarfed by the vast Victorian infirmary that was its neighbour. The weather was clear, and a thin coating of new snow lay on the ground. The slim trees planted in the cathedral precinct were bare of leaves.

They went into the cathedral and down the nave with its soaring stone arches and vaulted roof high above. There was a scattering of people inside, mostly older folk. Jeanne showed Sheila the ornately carved entrance to the Quire and pointed to the flights of stairs on either side.

"Down here," she said. "I found it yesterday. No one will disturb us."

Jeanne led the way to a deserted chapel on the eastern wall of the Lower Church, and she and Sheila settled themselves into two chairs. "Now, tell me," she said. "You've had me on tenterhooks."

Sheila unbuttoned her cloak and slipped her hand inside the neck of her uniform. Slowly, she drew out a fine gold chain, attached to which was a ring with a small solitaire diamond.

"You're engaged!"

Sheila nodded.

Jeanne looked puzzled. "Marco?"

"Aye."

"But he's with his regiment in Europe."

"Aye. It's six months since I saw him last."

"Come on, stop teasing me."

"Well. This is what happened. During our week's leave after preliminary school, I received a postcard from Marco's parents, inviting me to go round there for supper. They gave me a plate of spaghetti and some ice cream, and then they handed me an envelope with a letter from Marco and this ring. It might seem a queer way of doing things, but Marco and I had an understanding that we'd become engaged once I turned eighteen, and since we're separated by the war he arranged it as best he could."

Jeanne put her arms round Sheila. "I'm happy for you." She looked at Sheila's face. "Do your parents know?"

"What do you think?"

"Well, you told me Marco and his family are Roman Catholic," Jeanne said. "So I suspect you haven't told your parents yet."

"I will tell them, but not for a long time. We won't be in a position to get married for at least three years, anyway," Sheila said. "We're in much the same situation as you and Keith."

"What are Marco's parents like?"

"Very Italian, although they've lived in Glasgow for thirty years, and very welcoming. It helped that Marco had told them I'm taking instruction in the Catholic faith, at St Mungo's church. I didn't let on that I've only been to one class so far." She laughed. "Can you imagine me a good Catholic wife, and with an Italian ma-in-law?"

"It does require a wee stretch of the imagination," Jeanne said. "But you've got plenty of time."

Sheila tucked the ring under her uniform again. "I've been hogging the attention. You said you had news too."

"Aye, I've heard from Keith." Jeanne pulled out a letter. "This arrived yesterday."

"Where is he?"

"In a cold place where you never see the sun in winter."

"Almost as bad as Glasgow."

"A lot worse probably. He said it's far north. He's been skiing, and he's bought a pretty woollen scarf for me." She sighed. "He says he's very well, but they always say that, don't they? Oh Sheila, I don't know when I'll see him again. I don't even have a photo of him. All I have is six letters I've read a thousand times, and a tortoiseshell comb he bought in Casablanca. Sometimes when I'm alone I take it out and open it up and touch the teeth with my fingers and picture him running the comb through his hair."

"Imagine Keith and Marco both here in Glasgow, dashing in

their uniforms," Sheila said. "And the four of us dancing at the Locarno, you and me all dolled up."

"Keith and I have never even danced together. I'm sure he knows how. He's light on his feet." Jeanne folded up the letter and tucked it away again. "I'll write to him tonight. At least our letters reach each other eventually."

"Everyone is saying the war will be over soon," Sheila said. "Meanwhile, we've got each other. And a sluice room full of bedpans."

Jeanne laughed. "Aye you're right. Time to get back to the ward. I'm helping with dressings this afternoon."

Chapter 32

Norwegian Sea
February 1945

He was in a bunk with a lot of blankets on top of him and he could not move his body. Now and then he heard voices as he drifted in and out of consciousness. When at last he woke up, there were two men leaning over him: an ordinary seaman and a tall bearded man in a subaltern's uniform.

"I'm sorry we had to tie you down," said the officer as he unfastened the straps securing Keith to the bunk. "You were delirious and kept trying to climb out."

Keith gave a weak smile. "I hope I didn't say anything that might incriminate me."

"Not so far as I know. You talked about Jeanne, and a flag, and your father." The officer spoke briskly, with flat vowels that reminded Keith of Blue and Stretch but not quite. More like the exuberant character he had met at the Astor Bar in New York.

"New Zealander?" Keith asked.

"Bob Jones. Born near London, grew up in Wellington." Then Jones indicated the seaman beside him: "This is Mikey. He's been looking after you."

Keith propped himself up on one elbow. "Where am I?"

"On HMS *Zambesi*," Jones said.

"*Zambesi?*" Keith was puzzled.

"One of the destroyers escorting the convoy."

"How did I get on board? All I remember is being with my buddy Steve, and him falling ..." He shook his head, trying to understand. "Why did he fall into the sea? I hooked the line to his life jacket."

"His jacket either pulled off him, or it disintegrated. After he fell, he didn't resurface," Jones said. "It wasn't your fault. It was no one's fault."

Keith closed his eyes and tears spilled down on to his cheeks. After a while he asked, "How did I get here?"

"Lieutenant Jones climbed down into the sea to get you," said Mikey. Pride and admiration showed on his face.

Jones glanced at Mikey. "It was nothing compared with what these boys went through." He turned back to Keith and explained. "You no longer had the strength to move your limbs. Once we got you on board we were able to warm you up again. You suffered frostbite on your feet. The doc will have a word with you. Your feet will probably be okay, but you need to watch out for signs of infection over the next few months."

Keith nodded. "Thank you." He was enveloped in an enormous sweater, and he plucked at it, agitated.

"Sorry about the kit," Jones said. "We had to cut off your clothes. They were frozen to your skin. It was the same with the other men who'd been in the water. We rustled up whatever spare clothes we could find."

"I saved this for you. You were wearing it around your neck." Mikey showed a small leather pouch to Keith.

Keith was surprised. "I'd forgotten I was wearing that. An old seaman gave it to me in Halifax. There's a caul inside it, protection against drowning."

"Well, it must have worked," Jones said. "Along with extreme fitness and a bloody refusal to die."

A memory flooded back to Keith. "I saw you rescuing the navy boys and our commander from their raft. Where are they?"

Jones spoke slowly. "The boys are in their temporary accommodation, the petty officers' mess. They're very cramped. We all are. But at least they're warm. Mikey will take you there shortly." He paused. "I'm sorry about your commander."

"Is he all right?"

Jones continued. "He insisted on helping his men first,

securing the lines to the bodies. When his turn came, the line fell just beyond his reach. He dropped into the water to grab the rope but was too exhausted to keep afloat. He sank and we never saw him again." His eyes held Keith's. "He was a hero. You all were."

Keith tried to absorb what he had just heard. Eventually he said, "I'd like to go and talk to the others."

"Drink this first, then we'll get you on your feet gradually." Mikey helped him sit up and handed him a mug.

He coughed as the hot strong liquid hit the back of his throat.

"Rum and water," Jones said.

Keith took another sip of the steaming drink and then asked Jones, "Do you know how many of the others were rescued?"

"We saved about two-thirds of those on board. The *Opportune* picked up the people in boats and the larger rafts, and we went after the rest of you. Some of the men hung on just long enough for us to haul them on to the deck and then they died." He indicated to Keith to drink more of the rum. "We were lucky it was a relatively calm afternoon, compared with what it's usually like up here."

"My loader, Lincoln, a negro. He was in a two-man raft."

Jones looked at Mikey, who nodded. "Yes, we got him. He's okay."

"Where are we headed now?" Keith asked Lieutenant Jones.

"Back to Scotland. Those with severe injuries will be hospitalised, but I'm sure the rest of you will be put on a ship home as soon as possible."

"A ship home?" Keith was puzzled. "But I'll be h—"

"Home to America."

Keith paused for a long moment. Then he said, "That's right. Home to America."

Chapter 33

A week later, the *Zambesi* arrived at Scapa Flow, the huge body of water within the shelter of the Orkney Islands where the main British naval base was located.

The transition from the *Zambesi* did not go smoothly for some of the *Harold Beacon* survivors. While the seamen prepared to leave the ship by tender, Keith and the other Naval Armed Guard waited below, caught in a morass of red tape. They had no money, no clothes and no officer to represent them. Keith, still in a weakened physical state, felt mounting frustration. Although wary of drawing attention to himself, he was about to kick up a fuss when Frank Becker, the only merchant officer rescued by the *Zambesi*, suddenly appeared.

"Found you at last," Becker said. "We're ready to go ashore, and we just noticed you boys were missing." He busied around and managed to secure British petty officer uniforms for Keith and the others so they could board the tender.

When they arrived at Thurso on the Scottish mainland, the seamen were met by War Shipping Administration representatives and given some money; however, there was no US Navy representative to meet Keith and the others. The seamen offered to chip in for their train fares, but when the conductor heard this he gave the navy men free passage.

They travelled from Thurso to Inverness, where they changed trains for Glasgow. From there, they were sent forty miles to the Seabees base on the Rosneath Peninsula. Keith, along with the other navy men, was provided with clothes and pay and set to work sorting timbers.

Three days later he noticed that one of the toes on his frostbitten right foot had become infected. He notified the medics, and they arranged for him to be transferred to the US Army 316th Station Hospital just outside Glasgow.

Keith had drifted in and out of sleep, and now, as he became fully awake, he felt someone gently combing his hair. The sensation was so soothing that he kept his eyes closed. When at last he opened them, the woman who sat beside his bed gave a start and drew back her hand.

Keith turned his head towards her. "Jeanne?"

"Aye, my love."

"How did you know I was here?"

"You sent a message. Don't you recollect?"

"It's the anaesthetic." He shook his head to clear it. "I remember now. I sent a note with Dan Morbier, one of the merchant boys. He was in the same ward as me."

"He told me he broke into a locker to get his clothes and then hitchhiked into the city."

"Aye. A crew member had paid him a visit and said they'd soon be heading for Liverpool. Dan wanted to go with them, but the doctor said he wasn't ready to be discharged."

"He's a reckless lad, but he's arricht." She laid the silver and tortoiseshell comb on the small table beside the bed.

"You were combing my hair."

"Aye. It made me happy to do so. I'd wondered if I would ever see you again."

"Oh, Jeanne. You almost didn't."

Jeanne helped Keith sit up and poured him a glass of water from the pitcher beside his bed. "Tell me what happened," she said.

"The Germans torpedoed our ship after we left Murmansk. I was on a makeshift raft with Steve and Emerson. It was freezing cold." He sighed heavily. "Steve and Emerson both died."

Jeanne took a moment before she spoke. "I'm sorry about

your friends. I know you were close to them, especially Steve."

"That's the second time it's happened. My friends died and I survived."

She took his hand. "You survived for a reason."

He shifted his body restlessly. "Maybe."

Jeanne observed him closely. Then, in a lighter tone of voice, she said, "You should drink some more. The anaesthetic has made your mouth dry." She handed him the glass, watching as Keith took a sip. "Are you ready to give me a kiss now?" she asked.

"Of course I am. Take away this glass and come here." He gave her a lingering kiss and enfolded her in his arms. When at last he released her, he said, "That was very guid, but very proper at the same time. You're all covered up. You're wearing your uniform."

"I'm on my day off, but I thought you'd like to see me in uniform."

"I do. You're an angel, beautiful gleaming white. The nurses in this hospital wear a kind of light brown."

"It's the American Army Nurse Corps uniform. Brown and white striped seersucker. Verra modern."

He peered down the bed in the direction of his feet.

"Are you in pain?" she asked.

"Not really. They amputated one of my toes. Frostbite."

"Aye. I asked your nurse. Apparently the operation went well and you'll be up and about verra soon."

He chuckled. "Did you glean any more information from this nurse while you waited for me to wake up?"

"Aye. We had quite a chat. She's from Philadelphia. She said there's a nursing shortage in America, and I should have no trouble getting a job there once I finish my training."

"So you're not hoping I'll join you in Glasgow?"

She looked startled. "I thought you'd discarded the idea of coming back to live in Scotland. You said it was too dangerous."

"I don't think I said that, although it was unspoken between us. I said I had to get back to my ship. And now my ship's at the bottom of the sea." He saw she was listening intently. "As for what I did in Halifax—running away, I mean—plenty of other men have done the same. There are probably dozens of them lying low, right here in Glasgow; there's a whole underground economy. But—"

"But it wouldn't work for us, would it?"

"No. It would wear us down. We couldn't even go back to the village together. Sooner or later someone would recognise me, and they'd be judgemental."

"They would."

"There's an American troop transport sailing from Liverpool in mid-March. I'll be on that if the doctors pass me as fit to leave hospital. Otherwise, I'll be on the next one." He tried to read her thoughts. "Perhaps I'm presuming too much about you, taking you for granted."

"What do you mean?"

"It's more than two years until you finish your training, isn't it? Until you'll be able to leave Scotland and join me in America?"

"Aye."

"I won't hold you to it, if you think that's too long to wait, if you meet someone else in the meantime."

"Whatever gave you that idea? Remember, I'm patient as well as stubborn. And ..." She leaned over and kissed him on the lips. "Bidh gaol agam ort fad mo bheatha, thusa 's gun duine eile. I will love you and none other my whole life."

"Then I am ready for whatever comes next." He cupped her face in his hands and began caressing her cheeks, gently and rhythmically, over and over again.

Author's Note

Red Hill, Papakura
2008

It is early summer. There is a cabbage tree by the side of the road and I breathe in honey from its cluster of flowers. We are striding uphill now, past houses with shade trees, trampolines and other trappings of outdoor living. My father does not slow the pace— until recently, when the doctor advised him not to, he had timed himself on his walks.

I joke with him. "Slow down. I can't walk and talk at the same time."

He smiles. We have trod this route many times over the years, talking all the way. "Let's go as far as the Māori pā," he says. "Keep it from your mother." He must have seen a worried look on my face, because he adds, "Don't worry. If I get an angina attack, I'll just put one of my pills under my tongue."

Ten minutes later we have left the houses behind and are standing at the top of the hill. On our left is a fence with a stile that leads to a large patch of slim, dark trees and a rough path that twists uphill to Puke Kiwiriki pā. Ahead of us, the road dips out of sight to curve round the grassy crater of the extinct volcano that gives the earth here its distinctive red colour.

"I just wanted to see I was still able to do it," Dad says. "We could have gone even further, couldn't we? If we'd wanted to, we could have gone right round the hill."

We retrace our steps and are soon walking up the driveway to my parents' home. It is built of pale gold Huntly brick and sits solidly on a quarter-acre section. Fifty years ago, when the six of us moved into the house, it was clad in building paper (there was a delay in supply of the bricks) and the land was a bare paddock. Now it is densely planted with trees: redwood, puka, gum, maple, jacaranda, southern beech, tree ferns and liquid amber. The soil is rich and moist, and the flower beds a lush palette of colours that blend softly to the eye. My mother, Bobby—with bare feet and a dress splashed with poppies—is poised, secateurs in hand, in front of a hydrangea bursting with blue flowers.

My father and I sit down in the conservatory. The louvre windows are open and I can hear the soft cooing of doves and the hum of a car driving past.

"So you don't mind me having a go?" I ask, indicating the manuscript that Dad has placed on the table beside us.

He looks wistful for a moment. Then he says, his voice firm, "No. I don't mind. I was going to do it myself one day, but I'll never do it now."

Back home in Wellington, I examine the manuscript, a wartime novel that Bobby typed from my father's handwritten drafts when they were newlyweds in 1946. It is bound like a university thesis and has been edited heavily and decisively—whole paragraphs have been scored out. Tucked into the back is an aerogramme, and I recognise the sender's name: Warren Hart, Dad's close friend from his army and air force days. In my parents' wedding photos Warren is the best man, immaculate in dress uniform, just before he and my father were demobbed. Warren had difficulty adjusting to life in post-war Christchurch and returned to England for a short-term engagement with the RAF. The aerogramme shows that he acted as go-between with the J.C. Wells Literary Service, Fleet Street, on Dad's behalf, and he quotes their reader's criticism: *Much more could have been made of this story, which is also overwritten in parts … A careful study of the corrected script is advised.*

I wonder how my father felt when he received this letter,

and I plan to ask him next time I see him. But suddenly everything changes. Dad has a stroke, which blunts his memory (although not his enthusiasm for life). Six months later, he dies peacefully in his sleep.

Two years later I flicked through a fat notebook, the wartime journal Dad had given me along with his manuscript. In his notebook he wrote about training as a navigator in Quebec, his impressions of Canada and the United States, and his eighteen months in England. Two hundred pages in my father's neat, cursive hand. Then I opened the large manila envelope labelled "My writing" that Dad had given me at the same time. The contents included several pieces of descriptive writing and some letters. I recognised the sender immediately: Vi Spaulding. She and her husband, Art, were part of our family folklore. They were my father's American "Mom and Pop". Every Christmas my mother had sent them a card and letter. My parents had even visited them in Albany.

I read the letters in date order. The first was handwritten, with some words underscored:

Albany, New York State
September 11, 1945

My dear Charlie,

I wish you were here so I could <u>talk</u>; there's so much I just want to <u>say</u> and I find it more difficult to express myself by letter. But here goes.

I'm all <u>for</u> the story—very enthusiastic really—and I'll give you all the help I possibly can. Best you haven't met Frank McG for you can build your own "hero" as you really wish him and not be handicapped by Frank's shortcomings. He has them, you know.

Before you start (I'm advising "as shouldn't") it might be good to decide the "lesson" your work is to teach. There seems little room for a <u>moral</u>, for his actions were not exactly "right" from a military standpoint. But there are thousands who did as he did. Could you not take his life as a basis for your story, glamorize him a bit *without overdoing it, and leave him where he is today—his future a bit insecure due to circumstances, etc.? …*

You have little to fear from Frank. He's in no position to object and would not do so if he were. You will need to give him another name, of course, but apart from that I would change the story, but very little. Have him born in the Highlands (true); his mother dies when he's fourteen (true). He goes to London with his father (true) for whom he has no affection (true). He lives from "pillar to post", no care or attention from anyone (true) and finally leaves the paternal "home" for the army (true). …

I remember Frank telling me of an aunt and a cousin, Jeanne; of the outbreak of war and his running away to the army; of Jeanne's letters to him in Africa and how he would arrange them in proper order for reading when the mail would come after weeks without any; of the campaign in the desert and how they lacked water; how the dirt peeled off in layers when they perspired and how they learned to make their water ration last by a mouthful at spaced intervals rather than a good drink all at once; of throwing away equipment when the going got toughest; of lads going of bit mental etc., etc. (all of which you can get from those you know who served there).

Frank told me that he was a gunner on a bren carrier and suffered concussion when thrown from the carrier in a bombing. He told of being in a hospital recuperating from a fracture—his concussion is passed off as trivial—and then on a hospital ship to Canada.

This is all rather a muddle, I'm afraid. I will wait until I am back home with the typewriter and then write again with more details. But you have enough to get started.

This has been all "story". I'll write again with news of us. All is well here and everyone sends their love.
Sincerely,
Vi

So this is how my father's novel came about. There was a real man behind it all. I speculated briefly as to what his real name was—probably McGuire or McGregor.

In a second letter, dated November 11, 1945, Vi provided more detail about their experience with Frank:

The interval after Frank's first arrival in Canada is the one I have the least information on. He talked to me about it, but at the time he was still concealing the fact that he was many months beyond AWOL. As I remember it, the ship had docked at Halifax and was awaiting passage before crossing back across the Atlantic. Later he elaborated in this but I was beyond the questioning stage by then, being much too upset to remember all the details; a bit fearful as well.

So to begin again with the period when Art and I first met Frank. He came to this house with two very scruffy Canadians. The Canadians had seen service, for one was very peppered with shrapnel. It would be better reading to portray them as your devil-may-care Aussies, for they are colorful soldiers. ...

We asked F if he had any time left—he claimed to be on leave— and suggested he stay it out in order to rest up. He remained the seven days he claimed to have left and spent that time reading the books I brought him from the library. He asked for stories of the early days in New York State, of Indians, and the wars. So I got him "Drums Along the Mohawk" and the like and he would lie in front of the fire place with the book and a huge map spread out on the floor, tracing the story as he read and sticking pins in to keep the towns straight. He would even read all night, sleeping until well into the afternoon.

On the nights F did not read he would leave the light burning, shading it by throwing his shirt over it. He never left himself in the dark! This went on for the whole week and even on subsequent visits. When I got to know him better, I asked the "why" and if he feared the dark. He looked so peculiar as if he were at a loss and could not think of any excuse that would "get by". It was then he told me he heard "things" he was trying to forget, such as men hurt and dying; that he was not subject to this in the daytime or in the light but the darkness brought them on. Naturally I wondered many things that were not (then) my affair.

When he left he promised to try to get "down" (we thought he was stationed in Canada) again before he sailed. Well, he came back to say "Goodbye" so many times that I began to feel all was not well.

I must have begun to show my suspicions after about six months of this. I had learned to know him very well and felt it high time he stopped trying to explain "things". The trip before I had told him in a quiet way that I knew all was not well with him and that I was worried for his safety; that I had no idea of prying and intended him no harm but that it would be a relief to really know the problem and talk it over. He denied it at first but must have seen that he could not hold out with anything short of the truth. It was after this that he disappeared for so long.

When he came back he was in horrible shape. He was thin and grey and his face was a mess of sores, pimples and blemishes. We were horrified at the change and he told us the whole story at once. …

He ruled out giving himself up at this stage for he had been gone too long and seemed to feel he would go definitely mental in Aldershot. He said he felt he had recovered from the concussion. He no longer heard "voices" at night and could sleep in the dark. His eyes had returned to normal; before the pupils had been dilated at all times. He had acquired a resignment to things as they were but was hoping for a solution that wasn't too bitter.

There were but two courses left to him, other than turning himself in. One was to get to work, the other to get in service. One just couldn't walk the streets forever. It was well on into the winter and even American MP's would question his lack of warm clothing. …

First, after thinking things over, we talked of his getting a job. It could be done for he looked so very young. He ruled that out saying if caught, it would look as if he deserted to get the big money paid defense workers here in the States. He did not feel, too, that he had the right to safety when others his age were dying. That left but one thing—get back into service somehow. …

I am sending you for luck the little flag Frank gave me. He had it wrapped so carefully and presented it as if it were his one bit of home. You remember it as being placed at the top of our war map in the back room. Frank had it stuck in the dot marking Inverness. I'll have to remove the pin staff lest it tear this letter open. ...

I am also enclosing a few typed copies of Frank's letters. In my fear that some harm could be done him, I destroyed all he had sent me prior to his enlistment in the navy. So these will not give you too much help, although they may give some idea of his personality. ...

Best of luck. I'll begin to use your Christchurch address.

With love from all at this end,

Vi

There was also a third letter, written in March 1946, in which Vi answered specific questions from my father.

After a close reading of my father's manuscript, I realised I needed to do more than simply excise passages. Dad had ended the novel in a sudden and melodramatic way, with the main character and his sweetheart both being killed. Also, he gave no sense of what the main character was like before the chain of events that turned his life upside down. I began attending night classes on how to write fiction, and little by little my father's novel became mine.

Acknowledgements

The true story of a young Scottish army deserter who became a US Navy gunner on merchant ships was outlined to my father, Charlie Herbert, in letters sent to him by Vi Spaulding at the end of World War II. Mrs Spaulding was his "American mom" when he trained as an observer/navigator in Quebec under the Commonwealth Air Training Scheme. I used these letters as a source, and also my father's unpublished novel, *Judgement Suspended*.

In the latter part of the novel I placed my protagonist on a ship that departed Murmansk, Russia, in convoy in February 1945. For these chapters the following book was a valuable source: *The Last Voyage of the SS Henry Bacon* by Donald R. Foxvog and Robert L. Alotta (Paragon House, 2001). Some of the characters on my ship, SS *Harold Bacon*, are based on real individuals who perished with SS *Henry Bacon*; others are products of my imagination.

The research for *Deserter* took me across the world, and I found helpful information at the following museums: New York Historical Society Museum (WWII exhibition) in New York City; the Maritime Museum of the Atlantic and the Pier 21 Museum, both in Halifax, Nova Scotia; the Museum of the Northern Fleet in Murmansk; and the Russian Arctic Convoy Museum Project exhibition at Inverasdale, Scotland.

I wish to thank the Ministry of Culture and Heritage for supporting the New Zealand Society of Authors' mentoring programme, the NZSA panel for selecting me as one of the 2015 mentees, and my mentor, Dan Myers, for his wise encouragement.

Sincere thanks to my writing teachers, scriptwriter Donna Banicevich Gera, who got me started in 2012 through evening classes at Wellington High School, and poet, novelist and memoirist Diane Brown, with whom I studied online in 2014 through her writing school Creative Writing Dunedin.

I would also like to thank the friends who gave feedback on parts or the whole of the manuscript: Ann Marie Herbert, Chris King, Trish McBride, Val Meyer, Stella Milne, Tracy Powell and Roger Ridley-Smith.

Special thanks to my copy editor, Kathy LaVergne.

Many people contributed in small but important ways. Barbara Watson of Tri and Swim Fit confirmed that my opening paragraph reflected what she was teaching us; and Muriel Anderson, who served in five countries during the war, told me about nurses' silhouettes in tents.

Last but not least, I wish to mention two proud New Zealanders, both of whom were born in South Lanarkshire and both of whom were at primary school when war began. The first is my late husband Bill Barrie, who immigrated to New Zealand in 1954, alone on a one-pound fare. He remembered many things about the war, including being thrown out of bed by vibrations from a bomb dropped on Burnbank. Bill's national service was done soon after war's end, and he was able to give me the real McCoy on soldiers, scorpions, limericks and many other things. The second is Betty Houtman, who came here in 1949 and remembers people talking about the Arctic convoys and how dangerous they were. After Bill's death, when I had lost interest in my completed manuscript, Betty helped by asking, in her soft accent that was rather like Bill's, "Ann, I'm wondering when I'm going to be able to read your novel?"

About Ann Barrie

Thank you for reading my book. Here is a brief description of myself and my future works.

I was born in Christchurch but grew up mostly in the North Island. My secondary education was at Papakura High School here in New Zealand, and Kesteven and Grantham Girls' School in England. I have a Bachelor of Arts in French from the University of Auckland, and a Bachelor of Laws from Victoria University of Wellington. Over the past few years, since I retired from the National Library of New Zealand, I have become passionate about writing. My planned future works include the following:

Charlie Herbert's Writings: The War Years, 1939 to 1948. As an eighteen-year old university student, my father, Charlie, wrote a stream-of-consciousness account as events unfolded on the night of September 3, 1939. Later in the war he recorded his voyage to San Francisco on an American ship carrying wounded from the Pacific; his wide-eyed observations on the wonders of Canadian and American society; his sixteen months in Great Britain; and his return home in late 1945 on a troopship laden with Australian and New Zealand airmen. The final writings are about his first two years settling into married life as a returned serviceman in post-war Christchurch. Target publication date for this work is late 2017 to early 2018.

Searching for Margaret MacKenzie: The Story of a War Bride of World War I. My long-dead grandmother was a strong and mysterious presence in my life. A crofter's daughter with a restless spirit, she worked during World War I as a hospital nurse and then with Belgian refugees. She came as a war bride to a strange land, where she lived in public works settlements; then, as her health deteriorated, she experienced both pioneering private treatment and the public health system of the 1930s. Target publication date is late 2018 to early 2019.

The Deserter Returns. The story will be set in 1953. Keith and Jeanne are content in Montana when Keith has two visitors from his past, both of whom challenge him, and the action moves to the United Kingdom. Target publication date to be announced.